Rosanna J

Lorna Hill wrote her fir⸺ ⸺⸺⸺⸺⸺⸺
watching Pavlova dance in ⸺⸺⸺⸺⸺⸺
ten, discovered one of the ⸺⸺⸺⸺⸺⸺
that Lorna Hill wrote several more and soon they were published. Vicki trained as a ballet dancer at Sadler's Wells and from her letters Mrs Hill was able to glean the knowledge which forms the background for the 'Wells' stories.

Rosanna Joins The Wells, the eighth book in the series, follows Rosanna from the warmth of Italy to the cold of Northern England. Rosanna lives to dance, but her new family have other plans for her. Determined to become a prima ballerina she runs away and sets out alone to make her dream come true.

Sadler's Wells

1. A Dream of Sadler's Wells
2. Veronica at the Wells
3. No Castanets at the Wells
4. Masquerade at the Wells
5. Jane Leaves the Wells
6. Ella at the Wells
7. Return to the Wells
8. Rosanna Joins the Wells
9. Principal Role
19. Swan Feather

Lorna Hill

Rosanna Joins the Wells

Piper Books

To my lifelong friend
Antonio de san Giuliano
with love

First published 1956 by Evans Brothers Ltd
This new edition published 1985 by Pan Books Ltd
This Piper edition published 1989 by Pan Books Ltd,
Cavaye Place, London SW10 9PG
9 8 7 6 5 4
© Lorna Hill 1956
ISBN 0 330 29077 0

Printed in England by Clays Ltd, St Ives plc

Contents

Part One: ITALY

1.	Amalfi	*page* 7
2.	Rosanna tells her Story	18
3.	A Royal Command	26
4.	Papa Angelino	33
5.	Naples	40
6.	On Board the *Colonsay*	44
7.	Rosanna makes a Friend	49
8.	Gibraltar	56
9.	London	63

Part Two: ENGLAND

1.	The Waybridges	69
2.	Cyril	73
3.	Monica	80
4.	Rosanna tries to make Money	84
5.	The Free Class	89
6.	The Lace Dress	96
7.	Cynthia Roebottom visits Pit Street	105
8.	Ella at Covent Garden	112
9.	Life is Difficult for Rosanna	116
10.	The New Ballet	123
11.	The Blow Falls	130
12.	The Boy Next Door	132
13.	His Majesty to the Rescue	139
14.	The Evening of Ballet	144
15.	A Proposal of Marriage	151
16.	Rosanna Writes a Letter	154

Part One

Italy

Chapter 1

Amalfi

Amalfi is a little town situated half-way down the 'boot' of Italy, on the left-hand side. It possesses a beautiful *duomo*, or cathedral, round which the houses are clustered. It isn't a bit like an English town. To give you some idea of Amalfi, picture to yourself a pyramid of multi-coloured houses with flat roofs, sheltered in the rear by a semicircle of craggy mountains, and washed in front by the warm blue waves of the Mediterranean. Few of the houses and villas have gardens, but instead are hung with vines and creepers, and flowers grow on the walls, on the flat roofs, and in every nook and cranny of the old buildings. There is very little soil on this rocky coast, and so the people have made use of every little bit for the growing of vines, olives, oranges, and lemons. They have terraced the stony mountainsides, carrying up the soil on their backs in wicker baskets made specially for this work.

At the moment when our story begins, it was the hour of the midday *siesta* in Amalfi. The Piazza Duomo, or cathedral square, where most of the business of the little town is carried on, lay shimmering in the heat, quiet, as if under a spell. The market stalls were protected from the hot sun by gaily coloured awnings, and at first sight their owners were not to be seen. On looking closer, however, you saw that they were lying fast asleep in the shade cast by the stalls, or perhaps in a nearby doorway. The cluster of small shops round the *piazza* were closely shuttered. The donkeys dozed in the shafts of their carts and carriages, their long ears twitching sleepily to keep away the flies. The children slept in the shade of the fountains in the middle of the *piazza*, lulled by the sound of falling water, or in the narrow alleys, stairways, or tunnels that led off from the cathedral square in all directions, and by which you passed from one part of the town to another. The only moving thing on this hot June afternoon was the river Canneto, which flung itself in a series of milky cascades down the rocky defile called the Valle dei Mulini, which, being translated, means the Valley of the Mills.

On the broad steps leading up to the cathedral, in a patch of shade thrown by a stall of fruit and vegetables, lay a little girl of about ten or eleven years. She, like everybody else, was fast asleep, her legs, burnt to coffee colour, curled underneath her. One of her feet could just be seen sticking out from underneath her faded cotton frock, and it was bare, as were the feet of most of the other children. Shoes cost many *lire*, so why wear them, argued the Amalfians, when it was so much more pleasant to patter about on the warm cobblestones barefoot? And if the cobblestones were not too clean, owing to the dead leaves of fruit and vegetables that lay upon them, why, there was always the sea to wash them in! In fact, during these long sunny days, the youth of Amalfi tumbled in and out of the Mediterranean all day long. The *bambini* (of which there were a great many) could swim as soon as they could walk.

Suddenly into the *piazza* strode a young man and a girl. They stood there silently for a few moments admiring the picture made by the magnificent *duomo* with its great bronze doors, its façade of golden mosaics glinting in the sunshine, and its broad steps fringed by the gay little market stalls.

'Well, Ella,' said the young man in a voice that had a slight foreign inflection, 'do you think that perhaps *this* is where your ancestors may have come from?'

8

The girl laughed. She was very dark, and looked Italian, so that when she replied in perfect English it gave one a surprise.

'It's possible, but of course I shall never know. That's one of the advantages of being an orphan – one can pick and choose one's background and then alter it if one finds something one likes better! I've already chosen in turn Rome, Venice, and Milan as the places my forebears came from, and now . . .'

'And now Amalfi!' laughed her companion. 'Well, it seems to me that you might do worse. It is warm, at any rate!'

'It certainly is,' agreed Ella. 'A little *too* warm, I think!' She drew back into the shadow thrown by the tall houses. 'Oh, what a lovely *piazza*, with the fountains, and the old campanile, and of course the cathedral. And look, Josef, what a dear little girl! She makes a perfect picture lying there!'

'Yes,' said Josef, 'we Southerners certainly know how to relax! Do you know, Ella, if I was not with you, *chérie*, I should lie down there on the steps of the *duomo* myself and go to sleep.' He yawned loudly.

'Well, why don't you?' laughed Ella. 'I'll go to one of the hotels and ask them for a cup of tea. You can go to sleep, and I'll come back and wake you up at four o'clock in time to find Anya's villa.'

Josef bowed gallantly.

'Your company, my dear Ella, is worth much more to me than a little sleep,' he declared. 'I come with you to the hotel Santa Catarina – it is one of the best, I believe – and ask them for tea. Tea with you, Ella, would be to me as the wine of the gods!'

'Don't be silly,' said Ella. 'I know it's not true!'

Two hours later they were ascending the many flights of steps that led, by devious ways, to the home of Anya

Boccaccio, the famous ballerina. Madame no longer danced, of course – she was over seventy years old now – and she had retired to Italy to live because of a weakness of the chest. She gave lessons in ballet to a small number of favoured pupils, mostly the daughters of her friends living in or around Amalfi. When Anya heard that Ella Rosetti and her partner, Josef Linsk, were coming to Naples, she had immediately written asking them to come to visit her in Amalfi and to dance for her pupils.

'They do not often see such dancing as yours, dear Miss Rosetti,' wrote Anya. 'Do please give them this pleasure. I ask for myself, also, who am an old woman, one who may not see many more ballets.'

'Well,' as Josef had said, 'who could resist Anya when she begged a favour?' As a matter of fact, Josef might well have turned a deaf ear to the old woman's pleading – Josef had not much use for old women – but when Ella declared her intention of going to dance at the Villa Formosa, he had agreed with alacrity to go also. He liked *young* women very much, did Josef, and Ella in particular. Who knew what she might become? He could see her as a successor to Veronica Weston some day. Josef wanted above all things to partner a *prima ballerina*. So far he had just missed this honour.

After about half an hour's climbing they reached the Villa Formosa, less out of breath than most people would have been, since they were dancers. It was a large white house, of which Anya occupied the ground floor. It stood in a tiny *piazza*, almost filled by a large mulberry tree, which shaded it like a great umbrella. The windows had green shutters, and on the south wall an orange tree, bearing many golden balls of fruit, spread its gnarled branches. Over the porch, which was supported by cracked marble pillars, hung a flowering creeper, the fallen blossoms of which – some of them ten inches across – lay on the tiled floor like a gorgeous purple Persian carpet. From inside the house came the sound of laughter.

'They're waiting for us,' said Josef. 'It's just five o'clock.'

They went inside, and were greeted by Madame herself and a dozen or so of her pupils, who curtsied shyly, and murmured a few words in Italian. Then, after the two dancers had had a few minutes' rest, they changed into ballet costumes, provided by Anya, and began their demonstration of ballet to the students.

Meanwhile the *piazza* down in the town had come to life. As the campanile struck the hour of four, it was as if the silver notes had broken the spell of enchantment that lay over the sleeping square. The *piazza* was suddenly full of bustle and noise. Such a melodious noise too! Men shouting in deep, sonorous voices, women singing, donkeys braying, water splashing as the children pushed each other in and out of the fountains laughing and shrieking, the pattering of many bare feet on the warm cobblestones. The whole effect was rather like the opening scene of an opera. One expected at any moment a stall-holder to step into the middle of the *piazza* and burst into an aria! Even the black-robed priests gliding silently up and down the cathedral staircase had a theatrical look!

The little girl in the faded print frock was still only half awake when a small boy appeared suddenly beside her, and began to shake her.

'Rosanna! Rosanna! It is after four o'clock! Come quickly! It is time we went for the water.'

The little girl uncurled herself and got up, stretching like a cat. You could see now that, unlike most of the other children, she was an excessively thin child, with finer features than you find in most children of southern Italy. Her small head was set beautifully on a slender neck, and she was full of natural grace.

'Oh, it's you, Giorgio!' she cried. 'I didn't know it was so late. I must have overslept. It was so hot today.'

11

The two children regarded themselves as brother and sister, although, as a matter of fact, they were no relation to each other at all, the boy being Papa Angelino Menotti's sister's child, and Rosanna the daughter of one of his oldest friends. But for the last two years Giorgio and Rosanna had grown up together, and were inseparable, except when Giorgio went fishing with Tino and Giuseppe. Then Rosanna refused to go with them, because she didn't like to see the fish caught, a point of view that Giorgio found hard to understand, for of what use were fish if you didn't catch and eat them? Rosanna wouldn't even go to the 'lamp-fishing' and watch the sardines, gleaming with phosphorescence, swimming about in the clear water. No, there were some things about Rosanna that puzzled the less sensitive Giorgio. Then he remembered that she was only half Italian, the other half being English, and he shrugged his shoulders. '*Inglisa* – that was it!'

'Hurry, Rosanna!' The little boy was full of impatience. 'Papa will be home early today, you know, and we must have everything ready.'

The little girl pulled a nectarine out of the pocket of her dress, and began to eat it. Then the two of them ran off down the steps into one of the dark and narrow alleyways leading off from the Piazza Duomo. Someone once called Amalfi 'The City of a Thousand and One Steps' – a very apt name. Everywhere you go, you must climb either up or down steps! The stone stairs themselves are worn thin in the middle by centuries of passing feet. Some of them are painstakingly whitened by the people who live on that particular landing; others are dark and slippery with dirt and decaying refuse. It all depends upon the mood and character of the tenants.

As the children ran upwards, they could see, through crumbling archways and gaps in the wall, the harbour far beneath them, with the multicoloured fishing boats rocking up and down on the blue water. They got unexpected and enchanting glimpses of the vine-clad slopes of mountain and crag, crowned by the gleaming white walls of convent or monastery. Sometimes they took a short cut through a tiny *piazza* with a statue of a fountain in the middle. The cracked or broken marble basin would be filled with flowers instead of water. Flowers were everywhere. They grew in pots and jars standing by the side of doorways, on the roofs, in window-boxes, in every niche and crack of the crumbling walls.

At last the children reached the flight of stairs at the top of which were the three rooms that spelt home to them. At the bottom of the steps, in an alcove, was a fountain in the shape of a winged bull. Water spurted from nose and eyes, and fell into a marble trough below. Standing in the trough, and on the ground, were various pots and jars belonging to the people who lived in the tall tenement house, for this was their only water supply. Giorgio and Rosanna picked out their own vessels, dipped one of them into the trough (this was for washing purposes), filled the other more slowly under the bull's nose (this was for cooking), and staggered up the twenty odd steps that led to their home. They pushed open the door, and set down the pots on the floor inside. You may wonder why the door was not locked, but indeed there was little inside for anyone to steal. The furniture was almost non-existent. All that the room contained was an old carved corner-cupboard, a table, and one or two wooden chairs. In spite of this, it was quite a beautiful room. The floor was covered with luminous sea-green tiles, which reflected like glass, and tiles of the same cool colour were let into the centre of the table. The ceiling was decorated with paintings of fat cupids floating upon cumulus clouds. As a matter of fact furniture (or the lack of it) didn't matter a great deal, because the children, and also Papa Angelino himself, spent most of their time out of doors, either on the flat roof, or gossiping on the stone stairway, along with the other tenants.

13

After she had set down her water jar, Rosanna ran into an inner room, and up a further flight of stairs that led from one corner on to the flat roof that stretched outside their bedroom window. Here she began to take down a line of washing that she had hung there earlier in the day. It was now quite dry, and bleached to a dazzling whiteness by the hot sun. Giorgio began to set the table with an assortment of crockery, most of it hand-painted and exceedingly beautiful, for Amalfi is famous for its pottery and its tiles. Even the most ordinary things – like jugs and basins – were beautifully made.

And now the children began to prepare their evening meal of macaroni and cheese. Rosanna flung the handfuls of macaroni into a pan of salted boiling water, whilst Giorgio grated the cheese, and chopped the tomatoes. Then they set bread upon the table, with a large jug of goat's milk, and a hand-painted pottery bowl full of fresh fruit. They only had one real meal a day, and this was in the evening, making do with chunks of bread, cheese, and fruit at other times, and I may say that they never went hungry. They all (even the children) drank a sour, native wine, which tasted like weak vinegar.

By the time everything was ready it was after five o'clock.

'I shall just have time to run up to Giovanna's for some *sfogliatelle*,' said Rosanna to the little boy. 'She promised me some when I saw her yesterday. She knows how fond Papa is of *sfogliatelle*.' As a matter of fact Rosanna herself, and Giorgio too, loved the sweet, cinnamon-flavoured pastries that were made in a particular shop in Amalfi on certain days of the week. 'Are you coming with me?'

Giorgio shook his head.

'No – I'm going down to talk with Giuseppe about tonight's fishing. I shan't be long.'

They went their separate ways – Giorgio down once more to the harbour, Rosanna up yet more flights of stairs, along more white-washed passages, alleyways, and tunnels to the

14

part of the town where Giovanna Vittorini, her best friend (not counting Giorgio, of course), lived with her mother on the top floor of a tumbledown tenement house. Higher and still higher she climbed, until she could see, through gaps in the wall, the city lying below her in a brightly coloured mosaic of flat roofs, domes, and campaniles. And then suddenly she stood still, listening. Out of the windows of a tall house, surrounded by a high wall, floated the most delicious music Rosanna had ever heard. It made her think of cool water, and a little breeze softly ruffling the sea. It was (though she did not know it) Tchaikovsky's *Lac des Cygnes*.

I must explain that there were many different ways of getting from Papa Angelino's house to that of the Vittorinis, and it happened that Rosanna had never passed this house before, so she did not know who lived in it. She crept into the little courtyard, her bare feet making no sound on the carpet of fallen clematis blossoms lying on the tiles of the *patio*. Through the open door, she could see a large room, empty of furniture, except for a grand piano. At the far side were two long *barres* of polished wood, which appeared to be fastened to the wall, and opposite to them was a large mirror, in which the people in the room were reflected, so that they seemed twice as many. In the middle of the floor, which was made of wooden blocks, were two people dancing – a girl and a young man. Rosanna watched them, round-eyed. She had often seen people dancing, of course; in fact, she had often danced herself down in the *piazza*, but never before had she seen dancing like this. It was like the music, cool and flawless. The young-man dancer lifted the girl as effortlessly as if she were a feather, setting her down upon the floor without a sound, tenderly as if she were a spirit, rather than a creature of flesh and blood. Rosanna crept a little nearer, until she was inside the room, and everybody was so absorbed watching the two famous dancers, Rosetti and Linsk, that they never even

15

noticed her until the dance ended, and then the girl dancer suddenly turned towards the door and exclaimed:

'Oh look, Josef! That's the little girl we saw lying on the cathedral steps this afternoon.'

For a second Rosanna stood there, ready for flight – especially when the old lady (an old lady of quite exceptional agility, it seemed) ran towards her to 'shoo' her away.

'*Allez-vous en!*' cried Anya, who spoke English and French fluently, but, despite her name, little Italian. She was, in fact, a Parisian by birth, but had married a Milanese. 'Go away, leetle girl! No cigarette! No mon-ee! Go!' Anya had lived in Italy long enough to know that *all* Italian children beg – even the well-dressed ones.

Rosanna shook her head.

'I don't believe she *is* begging,' cried Ella. 'You're not, are you, little girl?'

Rosanna shook her head again.

'No, *signorina*.'

'You were watching the dancing?' persisted Ella. 'You like ballet?'

'*Si, signorina*,' said Rosanna with shining eyes. '*Molto, molto, signorina*. But I have never seen dancing such as this. You call it ballet?'

'You speak English?' exclaimed Ella, surprised.

'Yes, mees. My mother *inglisa* – English lady. She teach me the English good.' (In truth, Rosanna was fast forgetting the language.) 'I mean, she *taught* me English good. My mother, you see, is dead. My father also. They are both dead in the *frana* – the land-slip – when the mountain is falling upon our house in Majori.' Tears filled her eyes and rolled slowly down her cheeks. The ballet students gazed at her, horror-stricken. As for Ella, she knelt down beside the child and put both arms round her.

'Oh, you poor little girl! What a dreadful thing to have happened! Josef – Majori was that little village we passed through just now, as we drove along the coast. Why, you can still see the ruined houses. I wondered what it was.'

Josef nodded.

'Yes, I fancy someone told me it happened about two years ago. A storm brought down a large part of the mountainside, burying the village. Many hundreds of people were killed, I believe.'

'But to lose *both* parents – oh, it's too awful to even think about,' said Ella with a shudder. (She, herself, had lost both parents, but then she had never known them, so that was different.) 'And where do you live now?' she asked the child. 'And what is your name?'

'Rosanna Francesca Corelli, mees,' said the little girl. 'And I live with Giorgio and Papa Angelino Menotti in the Via Cappuccini. Papa is very good to me.'

'Well, that's *something*, anyway,' said Ella half to herself. She turned again towards the child. 'And you say your mother was English? Have you any relatives living in England?'

'*Si, signorina*. I t'ink yes,' answered Rosanna. 'They live in a place of the name of Hayfield in the north part of England. I see the address at Christmas time on the letters. Signora Waybridge ees ze wife of ze bruzzer – broth-er,' she corrected herself – 'of my mother.'

'Hayfield? Why, I know it very well,' cried Ella. 'It's on the outskirts of Newcastle – that's near where I used to live. Well, if you come to England, Rosanna, do be sure to let me know.' She said this more out of compassion than anything else, for it didn't seem at all likely that this little girl, living in the south of Italy, would ever come to Newcastle in the far north of England. Still, one never knew. . . .

'*Chère* Ella,' broke in Josef – feeling he was no longer the centre of attraction – 'if we are to catch our bus . . .'

'Goodness, yes – it's nearly six o'clock,' cried Ella. 'And we mustn't miss it. I think it's the last one. Goodbye, Rosanna – I must run and change. Take this, and buy

17

something for yourself to remember me by.' She thrust a note into the little girl's hand, which Rosanna didn't refuse, as an English child might have done.

'*Grazie, signorina*,' she said gravely. '*Addio, signorina*,' and pattered swiftly out of the house, through the courtyard, and away down the steps towards her home. Six o'clock! It was much, much later than she had thought. Papa would be home by now and wanting his supper, and Giorgio too. It was quite too late to visit Giovanna.

On a flat piece of ground between two flights of stairs Rosanna opened her brown little hand and looked at the note the English lady had given her. It was for ten thousand *lire!* Never in her short life had Rosanna possessed so much money! An idea formed in her mind, an idea which refused to be banished. She put the note carefully away in her pocket.

Chapter 2

Rosanna tells her Story

The next day at the same time Rosanna climbed again up to the quiet villa on the mountainside, and again she heard the cool music and saw the students dancing. Anya saw her too, but said nothing. Something in the little girl's face stopped her from driving her away, as she certainly would any other child. For a week at the same hour Rosanna toiled up the steps, and stood just inside the door, watching and listening, and then one day she took her courage in her hands and went towards Anya.

18

'Please, *signora* . . .'

'*Qu'est-ce que c'est que ça?*' asked the old lady, tapping the polished floor with her stick. (Rosanna had noticed that while she taught, she used it to point out to her pupils their faults, tapping their limbs gently with it.) 'What is it?'

'Could you – would you teach me to dance, *signora*?' asked Rosanna, while the line of students resting on the long *barres* nudged each other in amusement. 'For this?' and she held out the ten-thousand *lire* note.

Anya did not laugh, as she might well have done, since her lessons cost nearly that amount each. She did not even smile. She folded the note back into Rosanna's hand, and stared down at her thoughtfully.

'And so you want to dance as much as all that?' she said.

'*Si, si, signora,*' said Rosanna breathlessly.

'I cannot teach you for your ten-thousand *lire* note, my child,' said Anya, almost to herself, 'but I might well teach you for nothing.' She drew the child to a wooden bench and sat her down upon it. Then, to Rosanna's astonishment, she began to examine her feet, talking to herself all the time.

'Ah – so dirty! But strong, all the same. And insteps undeveloped, of course, but elegant. *Ça va bien!* It goes well – very well!' She turned to the child. 'And you will come here to me each day at this hour, *mignon*, seventeen hours until eighteen? You practise hard, yes?'

'*Si, signora,*' said Rosanna with shining eyes.

'Well, then, I will teach you how to dance,' said Anya.

And this was how it came about that little Rosanna Corelli began her ballet lessons. With the ten-thousand *lire* note (which Anya steadily refused to accept) she went to Naples in the bus and bought herself a pair of ballet-shoes – not blocked ones, of course (it would be a long time before Anya let her new pupil dance *en pointe*), but soft *demi-pointe* shoes. From five o'clock to six each day she toiled up the steep steps to the Villa Formosa, and practised her *pliés*, her *battements*, and her *portes de bras*, just as any other little

19

ballet-student practises them in every country in the world, for the art of ballet is universal.

At first the other students shunned her, for they were all well born, with plenty of money, and there is a great gulf in Italy between rich and poor, but gradually they came to accept her. For one thing, her dancing soon became beautiful to watch. She seemed to possess a natural gift for it, and before very long had outstripped the best of them. Anya watched her new pupil with a sense of great satisfaction. Here, she felt, was a little girl who would one day become a great dancer, and it had been granted to *her*, Anya Boccaccio, to discover her. She often wondered who and what the child's parents had been, and determined to ask her about them in the near future.

One day she paused outside the studio, listening. Someone was playing the piano, and playing it very well indeed. On going into the room, she found Rosanna perched on the piano-stool.

'Oh, it is you, *ma petite*,' said Anya. 'I did not know that you could play the pianoforte. Tell me, who has taught you to do this?'

'Mamma,' said Rosanna. 'My own dear, dear mamma.' Her eyes began to fill with tears at the thought of her.

'Tell me about your mamma,' said Anya, drawing the child close to her, and Rosanna, feeling she had found a friend in Anya, told her everything.

The Corellis, it seemed, had lived in a little white villa at the foot of a great rocky cliff in the tiny village of Majori, a few miles to the east of Amalfi. Antonio Corelli was an artist, and so the walls of the Corellis' living-room were covered with his pictures. They were mostly views of the beautiful 'Divina Costiera', as the stretch of coastline between Amalfi and Salerno is called, for he had made his living by selling his pictures to the tourists who visit Amalfi and its neighbouring villages in the spring and early summer. Like most artists, he was prodigal with his money (when he had any), so during the summer the Corellis had lived like princes, while in the winter, well, it wouldn't be correct to say that they had starved, because no one went hungry on that beautiful, fertile strip of coastline, but we will say they had lived more frugally.

The Corellis had been a happy family. All through the long summer days the villa had lain dreaming under the blue Italian skies, its walls washed by the warm sunlit waves of the Mediterranean. In the winter (which was about as cold as our English summer) Rosanna, after she had come home from school, had sat at her mother's knee and listened to Hans Andersen's fairy-tales, which Alice, her fair-haired English mother, told her, sometimes in English, sometimes in Italian. They had sung songs together – all three of them – Italian lullabies and English folk-songs (all about 'The Lass with the Delicate Air', and 'My Boy Billy'), and nursery rhymes, and very strange it must have sounded, had you passed by the Villa Amore, to hear 'Ba-Ba Black Sheep' floating out of the door, for there were no sheep on the Divina Costiera – only goats!

Presently Rosanna, following her mother's example, had begun to finger the keys of the little rosewood piano that belonged to Alice, and had come all the way from her home in the north of England, and which was polished each day with such loving care. It hadn't been long before the child, under her mother's careful teaching, had mastered the rudiments of the piano. When she was only eight years old she knew more about harmony and counterpoint than most people three times that age. Strangely enough she hadn't shown any signs of artistic ability. She had watched her father paint, of course, and was quick to criticise, but she herself had never wanted to paint. But perhaps it was not so strange after all, thought Anya, as she listened to Rosanna telling the story of her life. The child of a talented parent often breaks out in quite a different direction. The daughter of a concert pianist becomes an artist, whilst the

21

son of a *ballerina* turns into a singer. It was evidently to be like this with Rosanna – her father's and mother's gifts were to come out in her dancing. As the story went on, Anya became more and more sure of it.

One beautiful spring day tragedy had struck the happy Corelli family. The snows were melting from the tops of the mountains, and the air was already becoming warm. Rosanna had been sent up to a little village called Pogerola by way of a mountain stairway, which wound up the Valle dei Mulini, to deliver a letter to an English gentleman – a Mr Lansdowne – who was staying there. It was to say that the portrait Antonio was painting him was all but finished, and would he go down to the villa for a final sitting. Just as she had reached the village, a violent storm had arisen and swept over the Divina Costiera, rain and hail had descended in sheets, and the dried-up river beds had turned into foaming torrents. The Canneto had overflowed its banks, so that it had been impossible for Rosanna to return the way she had come, making it necessary for her to stay up at Pogerola for the night, and to this she owed her life.

During the early morning ashen-faced villagers from Majori and Attrani had arrived, telling of a night of terror during which whole houses had collapsed and been swept away. In fact the greater part of Majori had been engulfed by a huge land-slide. A mighty river of mud and water had roared down the mountainside, overtaking the people as they tried to save their belongings from the doomed houses, and the dead were numbered by hundreds. Many of them were children who had been in bed and asleep when the tragedy had occurred.

'Papa and Mamma?' Rosanna had whispered, white-faced. She had of course been awakened by the uproar.

The newcomers had crossed themselves, and several women had wept. The Villa Amore, it seemed, had been in the direct path of the avalanche. Its walls had gone down like match-board; the little rosewood piano had been smashed to splinters. Even Antonio's pictures had vanished. Only one remained, and that, strangely enough, was the unfinished portrait of Mr Lansdowne. Under the wreckage of the house they had found Alice, her face serene and untouched, with not even a smear of mud upon it. They never found Antonio. It was thought that he had been washed into the sea and drowned.

The Roman Catholic priests, who have an enormous influence upon their people, and who interest themselves in their lives, had held a consultation as to what would be best done with the orphan. When Papa Angelino (who was one of the Corellis' oldest and dearest friends) had offered to take the child and bring her up with his little nephew, Giorgio, who had also been orphaned in the disaster, they had nodded in agreement. Yes, it was a good plan for the *bambina* to live with Papa Angelino and the little boy – for the time being, anyway. In a year or so other arrangements would have to be made. It was known that the Signora Corelli was English, and had relatives living in England, but no doubt they were all Protestants. The longer the little Rosanna remained with the Faithful the better, argued the priests. And so this was how Rosanna came to be living with Giorgio and his uncle.

We will not say that Rosanna was miserable all the rest of her life, for that would be untrue. She was only a child, for one thing, and for another it was impossible to be miserable on the Divina Costiera, where every day the sun shines and the world is a beautiful place to live in. Besides, the people were too kind to her. Nevertheless, it is true to say she never forgot her mother and father. They were like a bright light at the end of a long tunnel, a tunnel which grew longer with the years, so that the light became smaller, though not less bright.

When Anya had heard the whole story, she stroked Rosanna's hair, and vowed silently that she would do what she could for the child. Her heart ached with pity for her.

23

As for Rosanna herself, she was happier now than she had been since that dreadful spring day two years before, when in a night she had lost both parents and home. Every day she had her hour of dancing in the cool studio of the Villa Formosa, and the Signora encouraged her to play the piano, and to study the pictures, and read the books in the other rooms. Most of the pictures in the studio were of dancers in ballet costumes. Rosanna never tired of looking at Margot Fonteyn, the English *prima ballerina*, as Odette in *Le Lac des Cygnes*, or Princess Aurora in *The Sleeping Beauty*. Another picture she loved dearly was of a little girl called Annette. (Rosanna knew this because the name was scrawled across the photograph at the bottom.) She had sad dark eyes, and she was dancing in a ballet called *Les Sylphides*. Her partner was a young man dressed as a Highlander in a kilt. Rosanna had thought the costume very strange, and imagined that the young man was a Greek soldier (Greek soldiers, she knew, wore skirts like that), but Anya had explained to her that a Highlander is someone who lives in the north part of Scotland, and that the kilt is the Scottish national dress.

Beside the door of the studio was a large notice where Anya pinned newspaper cuttings that she thought might interest her pupils. Rosanna learned from this that the Sadler's Wells Ballet was coming home to England from the United States of America, and would be visiting Italy in the near future.

'But not the *south* of Italy, alas,' said Anya sadly. 'They are to visit Rome and Milan.'

Another cutting said that Miss Annette Dancy, of the Cosmopolitan Ballet School, had refused an offer to make a film in Hollywood, and was shortly to become a member of the Cosmopolitan Ballet Company. Anya pointed her out proudly.

'She was a pupil of mine,' she declared. 'On the day that I retired she presented me with a bouquet of roses. My dear Annette! . . . And here is another cutting that will interest you, Rosanna,' she went on, 'for you saw these two young people dance on the day you first came here.' She pointed to a photograph in the *Continental Daily Gazette*. Below it was a paragraph which said:

'A beautiful picture of Ella Rosetti and Josef Linsk, two of Sadler's Wells' leading dancers, in *Le Spectre de la Rose*. They were asked to dance at the special gala performance of ballet at the Royal Opera House, Drobnik, during the week of festivities which celebrated the engagement of the young King Leopold of Slavonia to his cousin the Grand Duchess Sopheodorovitch of Lek. King Leopold was eighteen last month, and, according to Slavonian law, is now "of age". The royal couple watched the ballet attentively, and studied the dancers' every movement. King Leopold, we understand, had seen the ballet before in Switzerland, when he was the royal guest of honour at the Théâtre National, Lausanne. It is obvious that the betrothed couple are very deeply in love with each other. Their every gesture showed it!

'Incidentally, Mr Josef Linsk is a Slavonian by birth (a fact not generally known, since it is many years since he last visited his country). His father, Count Stanislav Linsk, was well known for his hunting parties, when many distinguished sportsmen used to stay at his hunting-lodges to hunt the wild boar that are still to be found in the wild forests of Slavonia.'

Chapter 3

A Royal Command

In her dressing-room at the Royal Opera House, Drobnik, Ella Rosetti stared at the sheet of thick, cream notepaper, upon which was engraved the royal coat of arms of Slavonia – golden wolves on a sable field – with a feeling of something like dismay. An audience with King Leopold in his private suite at the royal palace! To any other girl it would have meant the thrill of a lifetime, but to Ella – well, quite frankly, she was frightened to death at the bare idea of it! It was all very well to talk to (and dance with) a totally unknown young man in the snowy Swiss forest; all very well to dance before him on the stage here in the theatre at Drobnik (though she *had* had a vague feeling of uneasiness, and had half thought of refusing to come), but to meet the young man again, now that she knew who he was – *that* was something altogether different. The trouble was, she dared not refuse. Josef (who had not been included in the invitation) had declared it unthinkable. One just did not, said Josef, refuse the requests of royalty; one was only too honoured to obey.

'All the same, I'm scared to death,' said Ella to her reflection in the looking-glass. She took a last look round her dressing-room, and at the flowers that had been brought in by a page-boy and arranged in vases by her dresser, lining the walls (who knew when she might see it again!), and went down to the stage-door where the royal car was awaiting her.

She was driven swiftly from the theatre, and away towards the palace. The car was a large black limousine, lined with white, and there was a graceful silver vase of velvety white roses in a little bracket attached to the glass partition separating driver from passenger. They reminded Ella of something. Oh, yes, it was the bouquet that had been handed to her on the stage that night last year in Lausanne, when she had danced *Le Spectre de la Rose* before the young king and his suite. There had been a card with the flowers, and a broad white satin ribbon wrapped round the stems, and fastened by a beautiful brooch in the form of a little jewelled crown. She often wore it. In fact (she put her hand up to her throat) she was wearing it now on her muslin dress. She had arrived at the theatre in her everyday clothes, not knowing, of course, of the royal invitation that had been handed to her during the second interval, so she had thought it best to keep on her *Spectre* costume, a soft white frilled muslin dress, with pale blue trimmings.

After a few minutes, the car drove in through large wrought-iron gates, which were opened by sentries dressed in the colourful uniform of Slavonia. Ella remembered what one of her friends had said: 'My dear, the smaller the kingdom, the greater the ceremony.' It was certainly true! She was sure that at Buckingham Palace there wouldn't have been half the shouts of command, the clicking of heels, the saluting, and the bowing that accompanied her progress from the royal car into the royal palace! From a distance, the building had looked like a pocket-sized fortress, but on closer acquaintance it was quite large enough to strike terror into the heart of little Ella Rosetti (one-time Ella Sordy, of Pit Street). She wondered what the Grand Duchess Sopheodorovitch would be like, for of course the King's fiancée would be there, as well as other royal personages.

'Oh, dear!' thought Ella with a sigh, as she gave up her wrap to a resplendent footman (because she daren't do anything else) and followed another one along what seemed like several miles of marble corridor. 'Goodness! How I wish I didn't have to come!'

And then suddenly they turned a corner, and came face to face with tall doors of white and gold.

'Miss Rosetti, Your Majesty!' said the footman, flinging them open, and then closing them noiselessly behind her.

It was just an ordinary room, after all, even if it *was* a bit on the big side. There was no throne in it, nor were there any royal ladies and gentlemen in glittering court dress to look down with disdainful eyes on the simple muslin gown she was wearing. In fact, there was only one person in the room, and that was the dark, olive-skinned boy she had danced with in the woods of the Sauvebelin. He was dressed in the glittering dark blue and gold uniform of a Slavonian Officer of the Guards, but he wasn't wearing a crown. Ella breathed a sigh of relief. If he had been wearing a crown, she wouldn't have dared say a single word! And now here he was, holding out his hand to her, taking hers in his own and kissing it, just as he had done on that other day.

'Oh, but I ought to – I mean you shouldn't—' faltered Ella, not knowing what to say.

'I think that I fell in love with you at that moment when you so obviously expected *me* to kiss *your* hand,' declared the young man, just as if he were stating an ordinary fact.

Ella stared at him in dismay. But of course he was joking! And yet he looked quite serious. How did one chide a royal personage for saying things he shouldn't say? She decided to forget he was a king.

'You oughtn't to say things like that to me, you know,' she told him. 'What would your fiancée think?'

'Sophie? *That* for her!' exclaimed the young man contemptuously. 'You do not think that I care two snaps of the fingers for Sophie, do you? Why, I assure you she is a thoroughly vain and jealous young woman. And she has a temper, too, I can tell you! I am well aware of it, because she is my cousin, and I was brought up with her. Do you know, all during dinner tonight (the ceremonial dinner, I mean) she was kicking me under the table, because she knew quite well that I had injured my foot out hunting, and she wanted to hurt me still more. All the way to the theatre this evening we quarrelled. You must realise, mademoiselle, that the alliance between Sopheodorovitch and myself is a *mariage de convenance, c'est tout.*'

'Then you don't love her?' said Ella, deeply shocked.

'Love her? Hate her is nearer the mark! Yet hate is the wrong word. I could not hate anything so contemptible as Sophie. I despise her, and I believe she despises me too. She says I spend too much time driving myself about in high-powered cars, and not taking enough exercise. Exercise, ugh! It makes me quite tired to think of it. But let us not talk about Sophie all night. It is a subject that is quite distasteful to me. Let us talk of *us*. You must know, Ella, that had I not been a king, I . . .'

'Stop!' ordered Ella, so sternly that the young man did so out of sheer astonishment. Never in all his life had anyone dared to tell him to stop – just like that! He opened his mouth.

'Stop!' cried Ella again. 'If you say one word more, I'll go straight home.' She put her hand upon the gilded door-handle. 'I mean it.'

'I can see that you do,' said the young king. 'Please sit down, dear Ella. I promise you I will not offend again. Come, you cannot leave my palace all by yourself – you would get lost – and I am not sure whether they would let you leave without my permission in any case. Please sit down. You have my word that I shall not annoy you again.'

And now Ella saw that a table in a candle-lit alcove was laid for two – presumably herself and Leopold. A couple of footmen appeared as if by magic and waited upon them, to Ella's secret embarrassment. Her host, however, seemed quite at ease, and went on talking just as if they weren't there.

'Ah, you need not concern yourself about Guillaume and

29

Fritz,' he laughed. 'They are not human beings, but only domestics. One does not worry about such people. They will not repeat our conversation – they would not dare.'

With a throb of fear, Ella wondered what would happen to the poor man who was offering her an entrée on a silver dish if he *did* forget himself and talk. She wondered what would be the penalty if he merely dropped something? Probably a year or two in prison! There was certainly a medieval air about this palace, and about its master too, she decided, stealing a furtive glance at his black head when it was bent for a moment over his plate. Not that it was bent very often. Most of the time he seemed to be looking at *her!* He was a very strange person, decided Ella – half royal, and half just a rather lonely, frightened boy, who talked and laughed about the most ordinary things.

'Tell me,' he commanded, 'about those two girls you used to live with who gave you "what for". I think you said their names were—'

'Lily and D'reen,' supplied Ella. 'Well, of course they're nearly grown-up now. In fact, Lily has left school and is working in the Co-op.'

'*Comment?*' said His Majesty of Slavonia. 'Explain, please. Co-op, how is it?'

'It's a sort of shop,' said Ella.

'A shop! Ah, I know it now,' exclaimed the young man. 'A place like Harridges in London. But what a strange sounding name! I must practise it – Co-op, Co-op. I am learning plenty of English words from you, am I not, Mademoiselle Ella? First of all "what for", and now Co-op! And there was another one that intrigued me – you spoke about your *maître de ballet* "going up in smoke" when he was annoyed. That amused me much! I am often thinking of that when I am sad, and I have pictured to myself your face when you said it, and I have been forced to smile. Hans has tried to explain to me the exact meaning of it many times, but it seems to me to be obscure.'

'Hans!' cried Ella. 'Oh, I remember him. Poor Hans – he put such a lot of his money into that musical-box up in the Sauvebelin woods for us to dance to. I felt dreadfully guilty! Where is Hans now?'

'Oh, he is here somewhere,' said Leopold. 'I can never lose him for long. Hans, my friend, where are you?'

Ella nearly jumped out of her skin, when, without a sound, a large picture opposite her slid back, and out stepped a well-known figure – pale, middle-aged, dressed in black, and walking with a slight limp – Hans, King Leopold's bodyguard.

'I thought you would be within call, *mon cher*,' said His Majesty with a shrug. 'It is true that you stick to me closer than a brother!'

'Yes, Your Majesty,' said the other, bowing deeply at the same time to Ella.

'You know, Mademoiselle Ella,' went on King Leopold, taking not the slightest notice of the fact that Hans was standing behind his chair, listening to every word, 'never before have I met a girl who has for me such sympathy as you, who understands me as I feel you do.' (Actually Ella felt she didn't understand him at all, but it was true she *was* sorry for him. Although he lived in a palace and had everything he wanted, at the same time he had nothing at all. Moreover, he still looked desperately afraid, and jumped at the slightest sound outside the room.) 'Yes,' he went on, 'I feel that I have waited all my life for . . .' He shrugged his shoulders expressively as Ella got up. 'It is all right, my dear Ella. Do not distress yourself. I was just about to say that I felt we had met before, in some former existence, for I believe that we have several lives. I know you so well – indeed you are no stranger to me – that I am convinced I shall meet you again in another life, perhaps in happier surroundings. Of that I feel sure.'

Ella didn't know what to say. It never seemed to occur to His Majesty of Slavonia that there might be someone else she might want to meet – even in a future life!

They finished their meal, while Hans stood watching silently.

'Isn't he hungry, poor Hans?' asked Ella, just as she had done once before at the little *biergarten* in the Swiss woods. 'It must be awful to stand there watching us eat all these lovely things, and not to eat anything yourself!'

'Oh, he will have a meal later on, no doubt – will you not, Hans?' said Leopold.

Hans bowed deeply.

'When Your Majesty retires,' he said.

'Yes, and then he will eat it on the mat outside my door,' said the young king with a shrug. (He didn't seem the least bit grateful for Hans' devotion, thought Ella.) 'I call him my shadow, and it is indeed true!'

When the clock struck midnight Ella said that she must go. The car was ordered, a footman appeared with her cloak, and another carrying a huge bouquet of flowers, which he handed to Leopold, who in his turn handed them to Ella.

'I always think of you when I see them,' said her host. 'White roses for a white rose! *Au revoir, mignonne!* I look forward to seeing you dance again.'

And so Ella left the royal Palace of Drobnik, her arms filled with white roses. She was never to see it again. Three months later it was burnt to the ground by revolutionaries who had seized hold of the mountain kingdom of Slavonia and driven its young ruler into exile. The Grand Duchess Sopheodorovitch had publicly announced the breaking-off of her engagement to Leopold, and it was rumoured she was about to marry Ludwig Oppenheim, the new leader.

Ella read all about it in the daily papers – how King Leopold had taken the crown jewels with him, and also a large part of his private fortune, which was mostly in jewels also. (Hans was at the back of this, thought Ella. She was sure that the boy-king would never have thought of it for himself!) The papers went on to paint a heart-rending picture of the exiled monarch taking refuge in an obscure villa across the Italian-Slavonian frontier, pining for his country, and grieving over the loss of his dearly beloved (if perfidious) fiancée.

'Well,' said Ella to herself, 'he may be grieving for his country – I expect he is, poor young man! But as for the Duchess – I don't think he will be shedding many tears over *her!*'

Chapter 4

Papa Angelino

Papa Angelino, with whom Rosanna and Giorgio lived, was seventy-four years old. Papa Angelino had no family. He was a Milanese by birth, and quite a different type to the natives of Amalfi, who were short and stocky, with thick curly black hair, and dark eyes. Papa Angelino was thin and delicate-looking, with fair hair, and eyes of a faded blue. He was a gentle old man, and more content to listen to others talking than talk himself.

Giorgio, perhaps because he was a boy and not given to thinking overmuch, or perhaps because he was so intent upon his fishing, did not notice the things about their dear Papa that the more sensitive Rosanna noticed – that his steps grew slower and more hesitating, that he halted many times when climbing up the crumbling flights of steps to their tenement home.

'Wait! Wait, Papa!' Rosanna would cry from the top of the stairs. 'I'll come and help you!' and down she would run, her feet hardly touching the ground, so light and graceful was she. Papa Angelino would look up at her with great love in his old blue eyes.

'*Grazie – mille grazie, carissima!*' he would say, as he took her arm. Then together they would climb the remaining stairs. Rosanna would be very gay while they ate their evening meal, but when Giorgio was asleep, she would cry bitterly, for seventy-four years was not young, although, of course, many people lived a great deal longer than that – especially here in the southern sun, which was kind to old bones.

Meanwhile, the summer days drew to a close. The grapes were harvested; the lemon groves were covered with branches and dead foliage to protect them from the drying winds of winter and spring. School started again, and every day Rosanna worked hard from early morning till four o'clock in the afternoon. She and Giorgio attended the primary school in the Piazza Municipio, and great rivalry there was between the state primary school and the private school which was housed in the same square. The pupils of the latter turned up their noses at the children of the free school, and quick-tempered Giorgio had many a fight in one of the nearby alleyways before he went home. Rosanna had hardly time to be angry, for she had to run home, prepare the evening meal, and then set off up the winding stairways to the Villa Formosa and her beloved dancing lessons. She was by now far ahead of the other pupils, though she had only been learning for a few months. Very shortly, Anya was going to allow her to go 'on point', for her feet were as strong as steel, owing to much running up and down steps.

It was exceptionally cold that winter, and streaks of snow appeared quite low down on the mountain slopes. One day there was a scattering of it in Amalfi itself. The children

34

pointed it out to each other in great excitement – some of them had never seen snow before.

Spring came late to Amalfi that year, but when it did come it made up for its tardiness by the beauty of its flowers. The houses were almost hidden behind masses of purple clematis, mauve wistaria, delicate mock-orange, a riot of scarlet bougainvillæa. The scent was almost over-powering. It was indeed a delightful time of the year – warm, but not too hot. The first of the tourists began to arrive, the sleepy little shops opened up and set out their wares on the sunny pavements, or on little tables or benches outside their windows – ivory cameos in the form of brooches, pendants, or rings, strings of delicately coloured and exquisitely cut beads from Venice, lace from Sorrento. And, of course, everywhere you looked you saw the wonderful hand-painted pottery for which Amalfi is famous.

The spring lasted all too short a time, and now it was summer again. Rosanna was twelve by now, and had grown into a slender, small-boned, dark-eyed girl. Giorgio, the same age, had outstripped her – in width, anyway! Italian children are usually handsome, but Giorgio was exception-ally so. He had brilliant, dark eyes, a flashing smile, and a mop of dark curls. His limbs were straight and well formed, and tanned by the sun to the colour of rich mahogany. He and Rosanna had obtained a contract to give a display of Spanish dancing each lunch hour at the Hotel Santa Lucia on the cliff top, to provide a bit of excitement for the tourists who came by special buses daily from Naples during the spring and summer. Beside Giorgio and Rosanna, there were two Spanish gipsies from Malaga, and two Sicilians who had come to Amalfi to live. Anya Boccaccio was all approval. The Spanish dancing was good for her pupil. It would help to keep Rosanna supple, and stop her from becoming 'set' and strained. So Rosanna learned from José and Juan to play the castanets, and to beat out intricate rhythms with her feet in what José called a *zapateado*. She danced to the music of a couple of guitars played by the two Sicilians, and although the dancing was gay, there was something infinitely sad and plaintive in the music. The hotel paid them nothing for their services, but they were allowed to make a collection afterwards, and on the whole they did very well.

'Oh, look at those two beautiful children!' the romantic English and American tourists would exclaim. 'I do think Italian children are just too beautiful to be true!' Here a shower of nickel coins would tinkle into Giorgio's cap, which he had placed upon the floor in a conspicuous position. He never wore it upon his head; it was kept for sterner business – collecting the money!

With the money she received for her dancing at the Hotel Santa Lucia, Rosanna bought a length of material and made herself a tunic, like the other ballet students wore. She also went to Naples in the bus, and bought a pair of blocked shoes, and a pair of castanets. Not the cheap, painted castanets that are put out on the stalls to attract tourists, but a pair made of polished walnut wood. These were her most cherished possessions.

Just as the winter had been unusually cold, so the summer that year was exceptionally hot, even for the south of Italy. In the middle of it, Anya declared she could stand it no longer, and off she went for a cruise on the Aegean to visit Greece and its islands. So the shutters of the Villa Formosa were closed, and no cool music floated out on to the languid air. The dying purple flowers of the clematis drifted down upon the tiles, lying on top of one another like a rich carpet, because Anya was not there to gather them up. The orange tree in the corner of the tiny *piazza* dropped its golden balls of ripe fruit down into the garden below, where two or three sad-looking hens, imprisoned in a small wire-netting enclosure, pecked at them curiously, before deciding that they weren't worth eating. Whereupon a cloud of thirsty wasps attacked them, and soon demolished them. Occasionally Rosanna climbed up to the villa, just to be quite sure that Anya had not returned, but she was always disappointed.

During these long, hot summer days life seemed to stand still. You felt things would go on like this for ever. But of course life never does stand still (though it's true that it seems to move more quickly for some people than others). One day when Rosanna came down from visiting Giovanna and her mother, she saw a little knot of people standing at the bottom of the steps by the water trough, and looking upwards at their door on the third landing. A dreadful feeling of premonition came over her. Something terrible had happened! She knew it!

'Papa!' she cried. 'Oh, Papa Angelino!' She knew quite well by the way the people stared at her – silently, pityingly – that something had happened to him, that he was ill, perhaps dead.

And so it was. Papa Angelino had collapsed in the heat. His gallant old heart had slowed down and down, until at last it had stopped for good. He had not suffered any pain, said the neighbours, in an effort to console the distraught children. 'See the smile upon his face. It is just as if he has fallen asleep.' They did not notice until some time afterwards that Rosanna had disappeared. She had run up the mountainside to the Villa Formosa, quite forgetting, in her agony of mind, that Anya was not there. A storm had arisen, ominous rolls of thunder echoed round the mountains, and vivid flashes of forked lightning zigzagged across the sultry sky. Rosanna had run and run until, quite exhausted, she had fallen asleep in a corner of a ruined villa. The rain had beaten down upon her, but she had not wakened, and when she did wake, it was in a delirium. 'Brain fever,' said the doctor. 'Poor little girl! What a sad life! She must go to hospital, of course, where she can be properly nursed.'

Rosanna came out of hospital a shadow of her former self. She found that during her illness Father Bartolomeo, her father-confessor, had been busy making plans for her. Privately, Father Bartolomeo considered that God had taken a hand in Rosanna's affairs, and tidied them up very neatly. She could not (so argued the reverend Father) have remained much longer with Papa Angelino and the boy Giorgio, who was no real relation to her. Sooner or later the break had to come. Rosanna would have to go to England to her relatives, the Waybridges. It had better be as soon as possible, said Father Bartolomeo to himself. He did not, of course, know anything about Anya Boccaccio, who would certainly (had she been there and known of Papa Angelino's death) have offered to take Rosanna and bring her up as her own daughter – in which case this story would have had a very different ending.

'I have been in communication with Signora Waybridge,' said Father Bartolomeo to Rosanna. 'They are willing to take you into their home until you are old enough to look after yourself. You are a very lucky girl, Rosanna, to have these English relatives. All English are rich!'

'Yes, Father,' said Rosanna sadly.

'I have booked a passage for you on board the English liner, *Colonsay*, of the Global Line,' went on the good priest, who had indeed done his best for the orphaned child. 'She calls at Naples a week from today on her way from Australia. You will have to share a large cabin with several other travellers, but this, I think, will be more of a benefit than a hardship. I have ascertained that a daughter of Signora Carosio, who lives in the Via Garibaldi in Naples, is travelling to England on this ship also. She is to be married to an *inglese* who lives in Glasgow, and you will be in her care.'

'Yes, Father,' answered Rosanna, her mind numb with sorrow. Giorgio had been sent to live with another of his uncles in Milan, and she had been too ill to bid him goodbye; her beloved Anya had not yet returned from Greece. Rosanna felt that in all Amalfi she had not a friend. But this was far from true, as she found out later, when she left the little town. All the neighbours gave her little presents, and kissed and wept over her.

The night before her departure Rosanna climbed sadly up the mountain staircase to the Villa Formosa. Even if Anya was not there, she must say goodbye to the much-loved studio. She could always peep between the closed shutters! But when she got there, she found the shutters open, and Anya herself busily tidying up the little court-yard, for it was October, and the leaves were falling fast.

'Oh, Madame!' cried Rosanna, and burst into tears. When she had recovered a little, she poured into Anya's ears all that had happened – the death of dear Papa Angelino, her own illness . . .

'And now I must go away to England,' she added, begin-ning to cry again.

Anya said nothing for a moment. She had only come back the night before, so she had heard nothing of all this. She was sad indeed to lose not only her best pupil but a child she had come to love dearly. However, one must just make the best of it. Rosanna was very young. Her whole life was in front of her. Who knew but that it was best for her to go to England, now that she had the chance.

'There are schools of ballet in England,' she said (it will be seen that Rosanna's and Anya's minds ran in the same groove). 'Perhaps there will be one where you go. What is the name of the town where your relatives live?'

'It is a place called Hayfield,' said Rosanna. 'But I think it is only a village, and that there is a big town near called Newcastle.'

'Ah, that is good news indeed!' exclaimed Anya. 'In Newcastle I know there is more than one excellent school of ballet and one particular one kept by a Miss Mary Martin. You must keep up your dancing, and not forget

39

what I have taught you.'

'I will not,' promised Rosanna.

'And always remember,' went on Anya, 'that your dancing must always come first in all that you do, for I prophesy great things for you, Rosanna Francesca Corelli, if you work hard. Some time, when you become a famous dancer – as famous as our beautiful Ella Rosetti – you will come back to me here. And now, child, come inside and we will have a last lesson together before you go.'

Julia Spezzi, who usually played for the ballet classes, wasn't there, of course, so they had no music, but that did not matter. Rosanna carried the music in her head. She had not danced since her illness, and she was still weak, but as she danced she felt new strength flowing into her limbs.

Chapter 5

Naples

The Global liner *Colonsay* was not due to sail until six o'clock in the evening, but passengers were asked to be on board by five, so Rosanna was to go to the Via Garibaldi in the afternoon to meet Signora Carosio's daughter, Bianca, and they were to go together to the ship.

Of course, Rosanna had many times made the journey from Amalfi to Salerno, and on to Naples, but now, as she sat in the bus which wound round and round the precipitous coast road, she felt she might be saying goodbye to it for a very long time – perhaps for ever. The lovely little towns and villages appeared and were gone in a flash.

Attrani with its pyramid of white houses and villas, Minori clustered round its blue bay, and then Majori, where she had lived so happily for the first eight years of her life, and in whose little churchyard her mother was buried. The road mounted higher and still higher on the cliff, until the sea lay like a dimpled shield, hundreds of feet below. As the bus swung dizzily round each corner, the driver blew his horn, which had two musical notes – high and low. For years afterwards Rosanna heard the sound in her dreams, though while she had lived in Amalfi she had never even noticed it. Now they were passing Erchie, and Cetera, and were drawing near to Salerno.

The road between Salerno and Naples is flat, but in the distance rises a range of high mountains, on the upper slopes of which gleam the white walls and towers of many a monastery and convent, and more than one hospital, though how the patients are transported up there is a puzzle! The valley bottom is very fertile and thickly populated, and everywhere Rosanna looked she saw the peasants working in the fields. Most of them waved cheerily to the bus as it passed, and Rosanna waved back. They little knew she was waving them goodbye, she thought sadly.

The Via Garibaldi was one of the old streets that climb steeply up the hillside behind the magnificent waterfront where the liners dock, and which gives tourists their first glimpse of Naples. The Via Garibaldi mounted the hill in a series of broad stone steps, down the sides of which were open drains. The stairs themselves were slippery with dirt, and the tall houses leaned crazily towards each other, until at the top they were only a few feet apart. They were stopped from collapsing altogether by great iron girders, which spanned the space between, and were used as clothes lines by the inhabitants who were nearest to them. The noise, echoed back by the high walls of the houses, was deafening – children screaming, women quarrelling, men shouting and singing in loud, resonant voices, hens cackling

41

– yes, there were even crates of miserable fowls standing at the doors of many of the tenements – vendors of fruit and vegetables shouting their wares, donkeys braying, and above all the clatter of the people's feet as they milled endlessly up and down the flights of stairs.

Carrying her cheap, new suitcase (given her by the good Father) in one hand, the child soon found Signora Carosio's home. It was on the ground floor of a tall, ramshackle building. The Carosios' rooms were unexpectedly clean, though there was a large hole in the wall, which let in the daylight and also the wet when it rained. There were so many children in the family that it was impossible to count them, for they ran in and out like bits of quicksilver! Heaps of clothing and old straw mattresses lay in the four corners of the front room, showing where the inmates slept, but all the bedding was folded up tidily, and the stone floor had obviously been washed recently, for there were still wet pools in the hollows. The three steps down into the street had been whitened painstakingly. Above the door was the usual shrine, but there was a bunch of fresh flowers in a little chipped jam-jar inside it.

Bianca Carosio, the daughter who was going with Rosanna to England to be married, was sitting on the steps outside the house weeping, for she had never been away from home before, and who knew what sort of a strange, savage country she was going to? Her fiancé, whom she had met when the ship on which he was a waiter had called at Naples on its way to the Middle East, was now working in a hotel in Glasgow, and that city, she had heard, was not even in England, but much farther north. She was sure it would be infested by savages!

'*Mamma mia!*' cried Bianca. 'I almost wish I was not to go!'

'*Carissima,*' cried her mother, weeping also, 'it is best that you should. If, when you get there, you do not like England, you can always come back. Alfredo (as she liked

42

to call her son-in-law) will be welcome also. There will always be room and to spare for my *cara figlia* and her man!' Signora Carosio did not mean her remark to be humorous, as some people might have thought it, considering the size of her family and the accommodation inside the house. Many people in the Via Garibaldi had larger families than hers.

'Come, I show you somet'ing,' she added, 'and you too Rosanna Corelli.' She led the two of them up more steps, across a road, and into another street, equally noisy and dirty, then up yet more stairs, and finally on to a piece of waste ground where stood a bomb-damaged building. 'See!' she cried, and pointed through a gap in the crumbling wall to the harbour far below, where, looking like a toy from this height, lay a ship. 'The *Colonsay*! She docked an hour ago. Is she not a fine big ship?'

They stood looking down at the great liner that in a matter of hours would be taking them away from their homes to a new land, and Bianca, to her mother's dismay, for she had thought to cheer her up, began to weep again. As for Rosanna, she felt quite numb with fear and despair. At her feet lay the shimmering Bay of Naples, with its dreaming mountains, and the famous Isle of Capri lying like a cloud on the blue horizon, but she could not see them for her tears.

'Come,' said Signora Carosio, 'it is time for us to go, if you are to be on board the ship by five o'clock.' She was much more cheerful than her daughter, which was only natural when you come to think of it, since she had so many other children left to her, while poor Bianca was leaving the only home she had ever known, perhaps for ever.

Chapter 6

On Board the *Colonsay*

Rosanna had never been on board a ship in her life, and she followed Bianca and her mother (who had come to see them off) up the gangway, her eyes growing round with amazement. It was so big! Even the gangway – and there were several of them – was like a little tunnel, with canvas walls and roof. Bianca and her mother walked up confidently, for they had been aboard Alfred's ship many times while it had lain in dock at Naples for repairs.

At the far end of the gangway sat several officials demanding passports, tickets, and going-ashore passes, besides customs-officials and representatives of the various travel agencies. Members of the crew, with *Colonsay* in gold letters on the sleeves of their blue jerseys, were sorting out a mountain of light luggage which had been tumbled out of a net, swung over on to the deck by a crane. Rosanna's wondering eyes beheld a number of large cabin-trunks, besides crates, and boxes of all shapes and sizes going in through a hole in the ship's side. It was all very strange! Strangest of all was the ship itself. Why, it was like the Hotel Benevento, where she had once gone with her father to deliver a couple of paintings to a wealthy client. Her feet sank into soft carpets (carpets on board ship!), and there were real chairs and settees, like you saw in the windows of the furniture shops in Naples, all covered in rose-coloured velvet. The walls were decorated with flower plaques, all different, and all exquisitely worked in marquetry. Rosanna, being an artist's daughter, was so interested in them that she forgot all about Bianca and her mother. She quite jumped when a white-jacketed, peak-capped official nudged her arm.

'Wake up, kiddie! Your friends are going down in the lift.'

A lift on board a ship! The wonders multiplied every moment. She found, as a matter of fact, that there were several lifts, but they were all in the first-class section.

'Here you are – H deck,' said the steward. 'Cabin 73. If you want anything, I'll be somewhere about.' As a matter of fact, she never saw him again. He guessed from her appearance and Bianca's that they were not 'the tipping kind', so he left them severely alone.

Rosanna looked about her curiously. The cabin was very hot, though there was a kind of hole in the roof through which air rushed in a noisy stream. It was lit by a single electric-light bulb, for the tiny porthole did not allow much daylight to enter. There were six bunks round the walls, three of them upper berths, of course. There were two wash-basins, and a large wardrobe, the door of which was half open, and you could see that it was very full indeed. The only other furniture was a long bench-like table, with a strip of mirror above, and a couple of cane-seated chairs, over the backs of which hung several pairs of stockings obviously drying, and piles of magazines and books. These obviously belonged to the other occupants of the cabin, of whom there was at the moment no sign.

'It looks as if these are ours,' said Bianca, pointing to the two nearest bunks. 'You can have the top one, Rosanna – you're lighter to climb up than me!'

Meanwhile, Bianca's mother was fussing round the cabin, opening the over-full wardrobe and the bursting drawers under the bunks and table, and describing in voluble Italian the characters of the owners of so many clothes! You would have thought her Bianca had come out of a palace instead of the Via Garibaldi!

'But where to hang your dresses?' she exclaimed, throwing up her hands. 'There is not one single coathanger left! Nor one little drawer, either.'

45

'Do not fret yourself, *mamma mia*,' said Bianca calmly. 'I can always drop some of these people's clothes down upon the floor by mistake and put mine in their place.'

'Ah, that idea is a good one,' said Signora Carosio approvingly. 'My Bianca has the brains!'

After a while Rosanna left them, and made her way up several flights of stairs. The decks all had letters, she found. There was D deck, where the letter bureau and the shops were. The purser's office was on E deck. Rosanna didn't know what a purser was, but it was evidently something very popular, to judge by the crowds of people who milled round the office all day long. There was a huge dining-hall on F deck, and several lounges. Besides all this, there was a sports deck with a swimming-pool, and another deck where dances were held, and which was open in fine weather, but closed by sliding glass partitions when it was bad. There was a children's playroom, with a paddling pool all to themselves, and a nurse to look after them, and a library where the passengers could borrow books. This was all in the stern of the ship, where the tourists were accommodated. Through doors labelled in large letters in several languages, 'First-Class Passengers Only', Rosanna could see long vistas of deck (mostly empty), and long lines of chaises-longues (empty also). Occasionally she caught a glimpse of a first-class passenger, camera and field-glasses slung over his shoulder, leaning against the rail. There was a playground for the first-class children, too, and it was just above the third-class sports deck. Several beautifully dressed little girls came and stared down at Rosanna, then giggled and ran away. Rosanna had never thought of herself as a 'first-class' child, so she was not annoyed, merely admiring.

Suddenly a hooter sounded and a loudspeaker blared: 'Attention, please! Would all visitors not travelling on the *Colonsay* please leave the ship!' This was repeated at five-

46

minute intervals, whilst all the time streams of people made their way down the gangways, and other people dashed up them in a last-minute rush to embark. Groups of people stood saying tearful goodbyes to friends or relatives who were sailing in the ship and then hurried on shore. Signora Carosio came waddling along, accompanied by Bianca, folded Rosanna in her arms as if she were her own child, and wept over her. And then she was gone too.

At that moment a tremor could be felt throughout the ship, then a faint humming and the noise of swishing water. Rosanna ran to the side and pressed herself against the rail. The great ship was moving slowly, but irrevocably, away from the quayside. Naples was receding, the melodious sound of the Italian city was growing ever fainter, a light breeze had sprung up. Capri with its dusky cypresses was swinging round and away, and fading into the distance. A bank of pale cloud was covering the tops of the mountains, so she couldn't see them. She couldn't see them, anyway, for her tears.

'Goodbye, Amalfi!' whispered Rosanna. 'Goodbye, dear Italy! I'll come back some day, but it may not be for a long, long time, so don't forget me. I'll never, never forget you. Goodbye, my darling Madame Boccaccio!'

Very soon, all that could be seen of Naples was a semi-circle of coloured blobs, with a backcloth of mountains, their tops hidden in mist. They were so faint you couldn't tell which was mountain and which cloud. The *Colonsay* was at sea! And then, almost before Rosanna had time to dry her eyes, the loudspeaker boomed again.

'May I have your attention, please! Will all passengers who embarked at Naples proceed to their lifeboat stations for lifeboat drill. First-class passengers will please assemble on B deck, outside the games room. Tourist class at the end of the promenade deck.'

Rosanna looked round wildly.

'Run along, little girl,' said a middle-aged gentleman

standing near her. 'Didn't you hear what they said? Go and get your life-jacket. You'll find it under your bunk in your cabin.'

Rosanna ran along, down the various flights of stairs from one deck to another (luckily she was used to stairs!), but when at last she reached H deck, she couldn't find her cabin. All the corridors looked alike to her, and she dashed down one after another, only to find herself back where she started. Once, she found herself in the laundry in the middle of a crowd of women busily washing underclothes, and ironing dresses.

'Oh, please, could you tell me which is cabin 73?' she begged. 'This is the third time I've come down this corridor by mistake, and there's the lifeboat drill – I'm so afraid I'll be too late.'

'They'll never miss you if you are,' said a pleasant-looking English girl who was washing baby clothes. 'But if you feel you ought to put in an appearance, cabin number 73 is at the end of the corridor parallel to this one.' Then, as Rosanna looked puzzled, she added, 'I'll come along with you, and help fix your jacket.'

'Oh, thank you,' Rosanna said gratefully.

In a few minutes she was struggling back up the stairs, bumping this way and that, but nicely cushioned by the cumbersome canvas affair she was wearing round her chest.

'Right along the corridor, up the next lot of stairs, and round to the left,' shouted the helpful girl after her.

Alas! Poor Rosanna got lost again, and found herself in the first-class dining-saloon, where waiters were moving softly from table to table, switching on little pink-shaded lights and putting out menu-cards ready for dinner. When at last she found her way back to her own quarters she was just in time to meet the rest of the passengers coming back from the lifeboat drill.

'Oh, well,' she thought, a wave of homesickness engulfing her, 'if the ship sinks, I'll drown anyway!'

Chapter 7

Rosanna makes a Friend

That night Rosanna was very miserable. Everyone seemed to have something to do, somewhere to go, except her. Most of the decks were floodlit, and people were playing games with great earnestness – things called bullboard, deck quoits, and another game called shuffleboard. Rosanna stood watching them, but she was too shy to join in, and anyway it was obvious that most of them were in a competition, and were striving to get it played off before they reached a place called 'Gib', where, apparently, some of them were leaving the ship.

Presently Rosanna crept away from the games deck with its shouts of laughter and climbed down a companionway to the deck below. Here a dance was in progress. The dance floor was outlined with fairy-lights, strung on wires, and the band (complete with crooner) was playing a tango, which seemed to have a lot to do with someone or something called 'Jealousy'. For a time Rosanna watched the dancers curiously. She had not seen a great deal of ballroom dancing, and the sight of these couples, all languidly swaying in time with the drowsy music, fascinated her. The wind had freshened, making the fairy-lights dance and sway, and soon the ship began to roll, causing the dancers to slither first to one side of the deck and then to the other. Rosanna had a queer feeling in the pit of her stomach, and her head felt light. She went out into the air and leaned against the rail. Suddenly she saw a ship, lit from prow to stern, floating, apparently, up in the velvety dark sky. As she watched it wonderingly, it sank down slowly until it was in the sea. Then up it went again; then down. It was just as if it was held on a string, and was being pulled up and down by an unseen hand.

'*Santa Maria!*' cried Rosanna, crossing herself. 'A ship in the sky!' Then her eyes became accustomed to the darkness, and she saw that the lighted ship was lying on the horizon, and that it was the *Colonsay*, her own ship, that was going up and down. Her inside turned over, and her head began to spin. Many of the dancers were hurriedly leaving the dance floor, their faces pale green, and the bullboard players had forsaken their game. Only a few passengers, to whom rough seas meant nothing, remained on deck.

Rosanna crept down to her cabin, which she found easily enough now, used as she was to Amalfi's tortuous byways. Her cabin-mates were already in their bunks, lying with eyes closed, and faces pale in the faint light that filtered through an opaque glass panel in the top of the door. The cabin was very hot, owing to the fact that the cabin steward had been in some time before and had fastened down the porthole in readiness for the storm that they had been warned by radio was just ahead.

Without switching on the light, and making as little noise as she could, Rosanna undressed and put on her nightgown, which was a nondescript garment of striped cotton, washed and bleached to a pale grey colour, reaching only to her knees. She climbed up into her bunk, without making use of the ladder provided, and lay there miserably. Her inside felt a little steadier now that she was lying flat, but a fresh wave of homesickness and desolation swept over her. No one in all the world wanted Rosanna Corelli, except perhaps Madame Boccaccio, and she was being taken farther away from dear Madame at every moment. Hot tears rolled down the child's face as she lay there, feeling the ship shuddering and straining as it forged its way through the mounting waves towards that unknown land called England.

She woke early next morning and saw out of her porthole a depressing vista of tumbled grey-green waves, capped with white foam, which flung themselves with a slap against the thick glass, and then ran down like soap bubbles. She dressed with a struggle, staggering from one side of the cabin to the other, and finally managed to climb up on deck, bumping along the almost-deserted corridors, and hauling herself up the companionways. She felt better in the fresh air, though the very thought of breakfast made her stomach turn over.

It was so early that there was hardly anyone about except members of the crew. She crouched down beside the rail, and let the cold wind blow on her face. A more miserable, homesick, and seasick child than Rosanna Corelli at that moment it would have been hard to find. Tears rolled silently down her cheeks, drying streakily in the salty wind.

'Hullo! What is the matter, my child?' The voice startled her; it seemed to come from up in the air. And then she saw that it belonged to a young man who was looking at her over the partition that divided the first-class passengers from the tourists. 'Come here and tell me what is wrong.'

Rosanna shook her head.

'I can't.' She pointed to the notice on the door which said, in a variety of languages, that first-class passengers only were allowed on the far side. 'You see, I am not a first-class passenger.'

'Oh, never mind about that,' said the young man, waving aside her objection as if it were of no account. 'It will be all right, I assure you. I shall see to it. Come here.' Something about him, and in the tone of his voice, made it impossible to disobey, so Rosanna got up and passed through the door which he held open for her into the splendid isolation of the first-class promenade deck. There it lay, miles and miles of it, scrubbed to a snowy splendour. It even *smelled* different from the part she had left! There were rows of chairs tucked away in sheltered places, but the young man hurried her past them, up a small companionway to a deck above, up another stairway, and finally through a glass door into a cabin of such splendour that Rosanna forgot her seasickness and gasped. There was a wide window, not a mere porthole, through which you could, when the ship rolled, get a wonderful view of the white-capped waves far below. There was a writing-desk, with a leather-covered arm-chair, screwed to the floor to stop it from falling over, a table with flowers in a silver vase upon it, also firmly fastened down. There were several other chairs, upholstered in white and gold. The floor was covered with a white carpet, into which one's feet sank. There was no sign of a bunk, so Rosanna supposed that the sleeping quarters were through a door at the back of the room. Soft music filled the air, the ballet music from *Swan Lake*. The young man took a step towards a cabinet, turned a knob, and the music stopped.

'Oh!' cried Rosanna, full of disappointment – for was not this the same music she had so often danced to at the Villa Formosa? 'Why did you do that? It was so lovely! Don't you know that it was the Odette solo from *Le Lac des Cygnes?*'

'You know it also?' said the young man eagerly. He switched the radio on again, and the music returned.

'Of course I know it,' cried Rosanna, a little colour coming back into her pale cheeks. 'I've often danced it. Madame says I'm not really ready yet for classical ballet, but she let me try the Odette *solo*, all the same.'

'Madame?' questioned the young man.

'Madame Boccaccio,' said Rosanna. 'She was once a great dancer, you know, but now she teaches other people. She was teaching me until – until . . .' Into the young man's ears she poured out all her troubles, and he listened to her attentively, almost gravely.

'And now I'm on this horrible ship on my way to England, to live with people I've never seen,' she cried, remembering her sorrows as she talked. 'And I don't expect they want me to live with them, any more than I want to go there.'

'Oh, but you may be mistaken about that,' said the young man. 'They may be people of the most kind and charming.'

In the distance came the musical sound of bells.

'That is the gong,' said her companion. 'It means that breakfast is ready. You will feel better after you have eaten. I always have mine by myself. I hate eating with hordes of people staring at me. I shall ask them to bring some for you too.'

'Oh, I don't think I could eat anything, thank you,' said Rosanna, wondering at the same time why he should think people wished to stare at him. 'I feel so very ill.'

'When did you eat last?' asked the young man abruptly.

'I – I don't quite know,' faltered Rosanna. 'Oh, yes I do; it was yesterday at lunchtime. Signora Carosio was very kind and gave me bread and cheese.'

'You mean you have eaten nothing since yesterday at midday, and then it was only bread and cheese? No wonder you feel ill!' He pressed the bell beside the door, and almost immediately a steward appeared.

'Sir?'

'Tell them I want my breakfast immediately,' said the young man imperiously. 'And this young lady will have some too. Please produce something light but sustaining. A milk drink, perhaps, sweetened with glucose. You understand?'

The steward, whose eyes were nearly popping out of his head at the incredible sight of a near-ragged little girl sitting on the edge of the white-and-gold settee in the King of Slavonia's stateroom, managed to stammer: 'Yes, sir. Certainly, sir. Immediately, sir.'

'Just a moment,' added Leopold. 'Find my man, please, and tell him I want him at once. You will find him, I expect, at the purser's office. . . . Now, sit down, child.' (Rosanna had got up, and was preparing to go.) 'Didn't you hear me order breakfast to be sent up for you?'

'Y-es, but I think I had better go back all the same,' faltered Rosanna. 'I don't think that man liked me being here. He looked very startled. Didn't you notice? You see, I'm tourist, and this is first class.'

'What in the wide world has that got to do with it?' demanded her companion. 'If I wish you to stay here surely that is enough, is it not?'

'I – I don't know.'

'Well, I *do*,' said the imperious stranger. 'You are lonely – so am I. You have lost your country, and I feel sad for you because – because of something that has happened to me. I shall tell you about it, not now, but at some other time. For the present here is our breakfast.'

A couple of waiters had appeared with a tempting meal set out on a trolley, and behind them a pale, middle-aged man in a black suit who bowed ceremoniously to Rosanna's host and murmured, 'Sir?'

'I shall wish presently to sit out in the sun' (the sky was clearing rapidly) 'with the *signorina*, and there must be no crowd below to watch us. You understand, Hans?'

'Perfectly, sir. I shall see to it,' answered the other. 'I shall see that no one comes to this end of the deck. Do you wish me to wait upon you, sir?'

'No, no,' said the young man impatiently. 'I don't want you hanging around. I can manage quite well for myself.' He began to pour out the tea. 'Leave me, Hans.'

'You do get things done quickly, don't you?' said Rosanna in admiration. 'You must have a great deal of money.'

'Money?' echoed the young man. 'What has money got to do with it? I am – but let us not talk about *me*. Tell me about yourself – about your dancing. You must know that I love dancing very much – the ballet, I mean, of course. I have two young sisters – about your age, Rosanna' (he had learned her name by this time), 'whom I have placed in a boarding-school in Lausanne in Switzerland. I chose this school, which is called Beau Rivage, because I happen to know there is an excellent *maître de ballet* (teacher of ballet), a man called Steiner, who visits the school regularly. So my sisters will be in excellent hands, and will learn to dance beautifully, I hope.'

'How old are your sisters?' asked Rosanna, as her companion handed her a cup containing some sort of milk drink.

'Fazia is ten and Gina is fourteen. I think Fazia will make the better dancer of the two. . . . You feel better now?'

'Oh, I feel lots better, thank you. The ship still goes up and down, but you don't feel it shudder up here.'

'That is because we are high up in the prow,' explained the young man. 'You feel no vibration here, and also there is no smell from the engines, and no smoke. You should always travel at this end of a ship, and always high up.'

'Yes, but I expect lots of people can't afford to,' said Rosanna. 'Besides *somebody* must travel at the other end, mustn't they?'

'Perhaps you are right,' said the other. 'You know, it had never occurred to me! But I was really speaking of *you*, my little Rosanna. What happens to those other people' – he waved vaguely towards the tourist end of the ship – 'does not concern me. . . And so you dance, Rosanna?'

'Yes, sir.'

The young man's brows drew down over his dark eyes in a fine scowl.

'No "sir" to me, please! We are friends, are we not? I am – let me see . . .' He considered the matter for a moment. 'I shall be "Leo" to you.'

'Leo? That is short for . . .'

Again the young man frowned.

'You must not ask me questions, Rosanna,' he said sternly. 'Neither must you ask me what the name is short for. Enough for you to know that "Leo" is the name I wish

55

you to call me by.'

'*Si, si*, Leo,' said poor Rosanna hastily. Never in her life had she met such a strange, imperious young man. Yet she couldn't help liking him for all that. He was sad too – she felt sure of it – but after what he had just said, she dared not ask him why. It was obvious he wanted her to talk about herself. He was a very strange person!

Chapter 8

Gibraltar

Everything now changed for Rosanna, and life on board ship suddenly became delightful. Every morning she met Leo at the door leading into the first-class promenade deck, and he took her to his private sitting-room, where they had breakfast together. Rosanna's cabin-mates were curious about the child's movements, and asked her where she disappeared to all day.

'Oh, I've got a friend,' explained Rosanna. 'We have breakfast together.' They didn't inquire further – they were far too busy with their own affairs.

During the day Rosanna and Leo would lie in deck chairs, which had been made ready for them by the silent Hans, who also saw to it that no one came near them to stare (though why anyone should want to do so puzzled Rosanna when she bothered to think about it, which wasn't often). At their elbow was a small table, and on it a jug full of iced lemonade and a large box of chocolates.

'I know how much my sisters – especially Fazia – love

chocolates,' said the young man. 'Will you not try one of these round ones – they are filled with nuts and raisins. I am told they are very good.' He was as serious about chocolates as he was about everything else. He spoke very little about himself, but seemed perfectly content to lie there and listen to Rosanna's chatter, as she told him all about her life in Amalfi and her dancing lessons.

'One day' she said, '– it was the day I first found Madame Boccaccio's studio – I saw a lovely lady dance. She came from England, but she had an Italian name, and she *looked* like an Italian. I shall never forget Miss Rosetti, because—'

'Miss Rosetti?' broke in Leo. 'You are talking of Miss *Ella* Rosetti?'

'Yes, do you know her?'

'She is one of my dearest friends,' declared the young man. 'Moreover, she is the lady I intend to make my wife, now that I – that things have changed for me. This is why I go to England, for it is there that she lives. How strange that I should have met you who have seen her dance.'

'I think a great many people will have seen Miss Rosetti dance. Madame says she is famous,' said Rosanna. 'That must be wonderful, don't you think?'

'What must be wonderful?' Clearly, for the first time Leo wasn't listening to her. His thoughts were obviously far away.

'To be famous.'

'That depends,' he answered sombrely. 'For some people, yes; for others, no.'

That night they walked on the floodlit sports deck at the tourist end of the ship, so that they could watch the wake made by the great liner. The water of the swimming-pool was bright green, since it was tiled in green and lit from below. Overhead, the smoke from the funnels streamed past them in white banners. They walked to the stern and sat on a seat, looking down at the path of silver left by the ship as it fled across the ocean. There was no sound except the thunder of the propellers churning up the water into a broad foaming river, glittering with phosphorescence. Once they passed another liner, alight from prow to stern; once a dark little tramp steamer, with dim yellow oil-lamps.

Suddenly the orchestra in the first-class lounge began to play, and the music was relayed all over the ship.

'Hans!' cried Leopold.

'Sir?' came a voice out of the darkness behind them. (Hans always seemed to be there when needed, thought Rosanna.)

'Go below, Hans, and tell them I do not like this music that they play. Say that I wish them to give us *Le Lac des Cygnes*, and after that . . .' He turned questioningly to Rosanna.

'Ask them to play the music for the *Sleeping Beauty* by Tchaikovsky,' said Rosanna promptly. 'If you think they wouldn't mind,' she added.

'What does that matter?' demanded the young man. 'If you wish for this music, you shall have it. Go and see to it, Hans.'

'At once, your— sir,' said Hans with a deep bow.

'And you will dance for me?' said Leo eagerly as they waited.

Rosanna nodded.

'If you don't expect too much of me,' she said. 'I oughtn't really to be dancing classical rôles yet, as I told you – main ones, anyway – but I do love them so much.'

In a few minutes the orchestra hastily concluded the selection from *Show Boat* that it had been playing, and the cool notes of *Swan Lake* floated up into the night air.

Rosanna got up from her seat, threw off her shoes, and danced there on the moonlit deck. The young man watched her every movement. Several passengers, who had ideas of coming up on the sports deck to get a breath of fresh air, were respectfully, but firmly, shepherded below again by Hans.

'You do indeed dance beautifully,' said Leo when she had finished the Odette *solo*. 'I shall look forward to seeing you dance at Covent Garden some day.'

'I've got to get to Sadler's Wells first,' said Rosanna with a sigh. 'But just now it doesn't seem very likely. Madame said Sadler's Wells was the very best school in the world at which to learn to dance. She said that Miss Rosetti went there, so I'm sure it must be true.'

'It certainly must be,' agreed Leo.

'But I don't expect I shall ever go there really,' added Rosanna. 'I was only dreaming.'

'Dreams have a habit of coming true,' said her companion.

Suddenly the music changed to the *Sleeping Beauty*. Evidently the orchestra hadn't the whole score of *Swan Lake*, but only selections.

'This is the Lilac Fairy's *solo*,' said Rosanna. 'Madame taught it to me as well. It's a great favourite of mine.'

So she danced the well-known *variation*, and the young man sat on the seat with his arms folded over the back and watched her. When she had finished he asked:

'And now, supposing we asked Hans to order the band to play the music for *Le Spectre de la Rose*, could you dance something out of that ballet for me?'

'No, I have not heard of it. Tell me about it.'

The young king of Slavonia told her the story – how a young girl returns from her very first ball, clasping in her hand a rose that has been given her by her sweetheart. She falls asleep in her chair, and the spirit of her rose jumps in through the window, and dances with her.

'Oh, that sounds lovely!' cried Rosanna when he had finished. 'I shall ask Madame to teach it to me.' Then she remembered where she was, and that there would be no Madame in England to teach her anything.

'I shall go to Covent Garden Opera House, the big theatre in London,' she said grandly, 'and I shall see Miss Rosetti dance it. Did *you* see her dance it?'

Leopold nodded.

'Yes . . .' he said dreamily. 'It was at the Théâtre National in Lausanne. That was when I fell in love with her,' he added simply.

'And now you're going to marry her?' cried Rosanna. 'Oh, how lovely! It's just like a fairy tale!'

Neither of them thought about Ella's feelings in the matter. Rosanna was too young, and His Majesty of Slavonia far too used to getting his own way!

The next day they reached Gibraltar. Rosanna gazed at it in wonder. So *this* was what they meant when they talked about 'Gib' and 'The Rock'! Well, there was a rock certainly. Quite theatrical it looked, as if it was cut out of cardboard, and was part of a stage 'set'. Rosanna and Leo stood at the rail, high up on their own private bit of deck, and watched the preparations going on below for sending the passengers ashore.

'Only those who are leaving the ship at Gibraltar are allowed to go ashore,' Rosanna told the young man with a sigh. 'I'm very disappointed – I did want to see the Barbary apes they keep on talking about. They're monkeys, you know, and they're quite tame. They'll eat out of your hand, and they've lived on the Rock for hundreds of years. Marcia (she's one of the people who share my cabin) says that when they desert Gibraltar, England will lose it.'

'You really wish to see these animals?' questioned Leo.

'Oh, yes, but of course it's quite impossible, Marcia says so.'

'Who is this Marcia to say what is possible and what is impossible!' said Leo regally (which was quite natural, after all). 'Nothing is impossible. Hans! Go at once and arrange for seats to be reserved for us in the launch, and also for a special launch to bring us back again.'

'Certainly, sir,' said Hans, with his usual bow.

In a few minutes he was back.

'In half an hour's time, sir,' he said.

'Good!' exclaimed Leo. He was getting a great 'kick' out of acting as escort to this unsophisticated little girl. 'You shall see your monkeys after all, Rosanna.'

Rosanna looked up at him with shining eyes. He was like a prince in a fairy tale, she thought, and when you came to think of it, she wasn't far wrong!

While they waited for their launch they watched a fleet of little boats, which put out from the shore and gathered round the ship like a cloud of gay butterflies. Each boat was manned by a couple of Spaniards, who held up brightly coloured silk scarves, handkerchiefs, shawls, and other goods for the people on deck to see. They threw up lines to the ship with baskets attached, and soon a brisk trade was going on, the passengers sending money down in the little baskets and receiving silken goods in exchange.

'Oh, how lovely!' cried Rosanna, clapping her hands. She had all the Italian's passion for bright colours. 'Look at that beautiful shawl with the long fringe.'

'You mean the dark red one? You like it? . . . Hans! you will get us that shawl, please.'

'Oh, but I didn't mean . . .' began Rosanna. But Leo took no notice at all of her protestations. In a matter of minutes, the gay shawl was round Rosanna's shoulders.

'Now I shall be able to show you a Spanish Flamenco gipsy dance,' laughed Rosanna.

'Should you not have some castanets?' asked Leo. The sailors in the little boats were doing a good trade with these. Many passengers (children especially) had bought one, or a pair, and were trying out their skill. Clicking noises sounded all over the ship!

Seeing that Leo was about to order Hans to buy her castanets, Rosanna said hastily: 'Oh, but I have a pair of

61

castanets in my cabin, thank you all the same. They are very good ones – made out of real walnut wood. These,' she nodded at the painted ones held up by the sailors, 'are not so good. The noise they make does not carry well.'

'It seems to carry all *too* well!' said the young man with one of his rare laughs. 'However, I take your word for it, my little Rosanna. Hans – we will not buy any castanets.'

'No, sir,' said Hans, solemn as a judge. 'I think this is your launch, sir.'

'Ah – then we will go. Come, Rosanna!'

That night, at dinner, Bianca remarked to Marcia, who sat next to her at the long table near the door: 'I was sorry we couldn't go ashore at Gibraltar. Alfred said I was to be sure to see the apes.'

'Oh, well, I shouldn't worry,' answered Marcia. She spoke with a broad Cockney accent, but was an Australian coming to England for the first time to visit relatives of her dead mother. 'I don't expect you'd have seen them, anyway. My boyfriend (he's an engineer on the Orient Line) told me they don't often come down to the town.'

'Oh, but they *do!*' cried Rosanna, unable to contain herself. 'The people have an awful job to keep them out of the houses. They get in through the windows. Leo and I saw several apes climbing about, and we fed one of them. He was sweet – just like a teddy-bear!'

The whole table stopped eating and stared at her. Then Bianca tapped her head significantly. The poor child wasn't well. She'd had such a sad life it was no wonder she was a bit odd, and imagined things. Oh, well, it was nice to see her looking so cheerful, and if she *thought* she'd seen the Barbary apes, well it was next best to *really* having seen them and a shame to disillusion her! She discussed the matter of Rosanna and her imaginings with Marcia over their coffee later in the evening.

'This "Leo" she talks about. Nobody's ever seen him. I

suppose she's imagined *him* too,' she said. 'The kid's for ever talking about him! . . . *Santa Maria*, but I'll be glad to get the *bambina* safely in the train! One never knows whom, or what, she will invent next!'

Chapter 9

London

The following day was their last at sea. Next morning the ship would dock at Southampton and the voyage would be over. Rosanna felt sick at the thought of it. For her it meant a strange country, strange relatives, and no friendly Leo to make her every wish come true. Had she been older she would have wondered about Leo – who, and what he was – but Rosanna was very young for her age, and she merely regarded the young man as a sort of fairy prince. As for Leo, he seemed to be determined to keep up his rôle of Aladdin (with Hans as the genie who carried out his master's every wish).

'How would you like to see a real ballet performance tomorrow night at Covent Garden?' he asked casually. 'I think you told me it had been arranged for you to travel overnight to this town – this Newcastle? I have ascertained that the night train does not leave King's Cross (which is the station for the north) until nearly midnight, so there would be plenty of time. One of the ballets tomorrow night is *Le Spectre de la Rose*, and the ballerina is Mlle Ella Rosetti.'

Rosanna was speechless with delight. Then her face fell.

'Oh, but if Covent Garden is like the Opera House at Naples,' she said, 'one would have to wear something very special, and all I have is *this*.' She looked down ruefully at her faded print frock. 'It might be all right if I were by myself, but not with *you*, Leo.' Even Rosanna had come to realise that the young man was not quite an ordinary person. 'Thank you very much all the same for asking me,' she added.

Leo considered the matter for a few moments.

'I will see what can be done,' he said at length, meaning, of course, as Rosanna knew, that *Hans* would see what could be done. 'But whatever it is, it will have to be completed quickly, since the boat-train arrives in London at about midday, I believe. That means we shall have only the afternoon before us. I think,' he went on, 'that you had better perhaps ask the friend who is in charge of you' (Rosanna had told him all about Bianca) 'to accompany us. She would not, I am sure, approve of you being out alone at so late an hour. I shall be staying at the Dorchester Hotel, so perhaps the signorina could bring you there in a taxi at about seven o'clock. Meanwhile I shall send Hans with you to do shopping. My young sisters always shop at Harridges in the West End, so he will take you there. And now I think it is better that we should say goodbye here. Tomorrow morning all will be noise and bustle, and I shall leave the ship as quickly as possible.' He held out his hand: '*Addio*, little friend.'

What Bianca thought, when confronted by Hans, must remain a matter of conjecture, since her friend Marcia had already left the ship, and she had no one to discuss the matter with. But certain it is that she began to think it was *she* who was suffering from delusions, and not Rosanna! The thoughts of the shop assistant at Harridges' Young Ladies' Department are easier to discover, however, because she entertained her friends later on by a vivid description of the whole affair.

'At first,' she confided to Helen, her bosom friend, who was in the Haberdashery, 'I didn't know who it was I was serving, and then I just happened to see the notepaper where he had written down the garments the little girl would need. My dear, I can tell you my heart missed a beat! On the notepaper was a crest, and underneath were the arms of the royal house of Slavonia. I recognised them at once, you know, because of that article in *Women's Life* called "Royal Love". And then, of course, I recognised His Majesty King Leopold himself. He seemed older than I thought, but I suppose care *does* age one in a night, so to speak. The little girl was obviously his young sister Fazia. We supply all her clothes, you know. After the first few minutes I recognised her too, in spite of the ragged garments she was wearing. I suppose they had to dress her like that in order to smuggle her out of the country, poor child! It's awful to think what these royal children go through! . . . Yes, madam? Girls' jodhpurs? You want the Riding Clothes, madam. Second to the right, at the end of the Hosiery. . . . What was I saying, Helen? Oh, yes – well, we fitted out Her Royal Highness from top to toe, and beautiful she looked when we'd finished. There's no mistaking blue blood, is there? You could tell who she was a mile off! She wore the clothes straight away, because they were going to the ballet in the evening. Yes, Covent Garden – *Le Spectre de la Rose* with Rosetti and Linsk. Wouldn't mind standing for the gallery myself if I'm finished in time. Quite a talkative young lady, the Princess Fazia! Told me all about her ballet lessons. Amazing how fashionable ballet is nowadays . . .!'

If we want to know anything about Rosanna's visit to the Royal Opera House, we can learn a lot from a paragraph that appeared next morning in the *Daily Clarion*. It was headed:

The Royal Box was graced last night by the presence of two royal personages – King Leopold of Slavonia, who arrived in England in the Global liner *Colonsay* only yesterday morning, and his young sister, Fazia (or was it Gina?). The young king looked pale after his recent ordeal. The young princess, on the other hand, was a radiant figure in a beautiful frock of white lace, which suited her dark beauty to perfection. Both she and her brother were keenly interested in the ballets, which were *The Rake's Progress* and *Le Spectre de la Rose*. Miss Rosetti's dancing in the latter ballet was outstanding. At the end she received an ovation. She is a very young and shy ballerina, and she seemed quite overcome by the tributes of flowers that were handed up to her, and laid at her feet by admirers.

The Princess Fazia was obviously delighted with this ballet (a particularly suitable one for children, if we may say so), and rose to her feet several times, clapping her hands. His Majesty seemed impressed also. Seated a little behind the royal guests was a buxom young woman who was obviously Tania, the princess's governess, who, we understand, also escaped from the royal palace.

One wonders what the little princess, used to the warm and sunny climate of Slavonia, thought of England, on this cold, grey first of November?

Well, we shall never know what the Princess Fazia thought of England, for she was, of course, far away in her Swiss boarding-school, but as for Rosanna – she thought England (or London, at any rate) the most terrifying place she had ever seen. The noise, for one thing! She was used to noise – Italian cities are noisy enough, goodness knows! – but the clamour of the London streets was something altogether different. The racketing tube, with its escalators and its trains, whose doors slid open and shut all by themselves, its streams of people all hurrying along purposefully, with grim, unsmiling faces and harsh, metallic voices (not a song among the lot!) – these unfamiliar things struck terror into the heart of little Rosanna Corelli.

Then there was the cold, misty air. It caught in her throat, and made her cough. Leo had put them into a taxi at Covent Garden, but had not offered to pay for it (indeed it had never occurred to him to do so), and Bianca grumbled all the way to King's Cross Station about the money it was costing her, when they could quite easily have gone in the tube, or by bus, since their luggage was there already. They were to travel north on the same train, Rosanna leaving it at Newcastle, and Bianca changing for Glasgow.

While Bianca grumbled at the taxi fare, Rosanna was busy with her thoughts, and sad thoughts they were! Leo had said goodbye quite finally, and she wondered if she would ever see him again. Since he had not asked her for her address, she didn't think it likely. As for Leopold, he never even thought of a second meeting with Rosanna. She had helped to relieve his boredom and loneliness on board ship, and he had given her what pleasure he could in return. Now he had bidden the child goodbye, and that was the end of the affair as far as he was concerned. But Fate has many surprises up her sleeve, and Rosanna *did* see the young man again – and in the most dramatic of circumstances, as you shall hear later on.

Meanwhile, she and Bianca had arrived at King's Cross station to find their train already in. It was not due to leave until a quarter to twelve, however, so there would be plenty of time for a hot meal, said Bianca. But alas, she was unfamiliar with English railway stations, and did not know that even in London the restaurants are all closed at night. One could get cups of tea, it seemed, at a trolley on the platform, together with packets of biscuits, and cold, unappetising pork pies, but the cold wind whistling through the station sent them shuddering for the shelter of the train, leaving their pies half-eaten. All the berths in the sleeping-cars were taken, so they resigned themselves to sitting up all night. Something had gone wrong with the heating system of the train, and the carriage was deadly cold. No wonder the tears began to trickle from under Rosanna's eyelashes!

So this was England! In Italy the English and Americans were considered to be rich and all-powerful – fortunate as gods! If (like Bianca) you married an Englishman you were lucky indeed, for then you would become English yourself, and what more could any girl possibly want? Rosanna, gazing at the depressing sight of King's Cross station on this chill November night, felt that all *she* wanted was to be back again in sunny Italy. No matter how poor she was, how ragged her clothes, or how hungry she grew, she had at least a blue sky over her head and the sun to warm her. Here – the train began to move out of the station, and the rain spattered against the windows – here it was terrible! Quite terrible! Moreover, there were the Waybridges, who were getting nearer every minute! What would the unknown Waybridges be like?

Part Two

England

Chapter 1

The Waybridges

The Waybridges lived in a semi-detached house in Hayfield, a suburb of Newcastle. When they had first come to live in Denton Drive it had been almost in the country, but now the town had crept up to it, supplanting the hayfields from which it had got its name.

Thomas Waybridge, a neat, rather insignificant-looking little man, was under-manager of his department in a big engineering and shipbuilding firm on Tyneside. The fact that he had got as far as he had was due mostly to the pushing propensities of his wife. She was a loud-voiced woman with fuzzy, bran-coloured hair and a florid complexion. When she had married Thomas, she had been determined that he should 'get on', so she had prodded him here, and pushed him there, until by sheer force of weight he had arrived at his present eminence quite without knowing how he had got there. In the same way Mrs Waybridge had pushed herself and family first into a council house, then into a terrace house, and finally into a semi-detached villa, complete with a garage at the side. The house had a small garden at the back with a summer-house in which nobody ever sat because it was overlooked by the house next door, and also by the one (not attached but adjacent) on the other side. In front was another small garden with a crazy-paving path which wound up to the front door, and on the far side a rose bed in the middle of which, on a stone pedestal, sat a stone eagle that glared at you challengingly as you opened the gate, much as Mrs Waybridge would glare at you, wondering whether you were 'anybody', or just a 'nobody' begging for the church, or selling things.

Of her two children, Bessie Waybridge (as might be expected) preferred Cyril. He was sixteen, a tall handsome lad with very dark eyes and a rather crafty smile. He was brilliant in a smart way, and had won a scholarship from the council school down the road to the grammar school on the hill. He was the sort of boy who would do well in examinations for he had no nerves, and who would always win competitions for he was quite ruthless. He had, moreover, all his mother's push and driving force. Cyril Waybridge would climb to the top, by hook or by crook, and would in later life be known as 'the boss', a term which would be no mere appellation! Monica (at fourteen) was a smaller, rather less brilliant, edition of her brother.

We will join the Waybridges at breakfast time on a certain October morning when a letter from Italy, addressed to Thomas in copper-plate handwriting, had arrived only a short time before.

'Well!' said Thomas as he read it for the second time, '*Well!*'

'What is it?' demanded Bessie, bustling in with the porridge. 'Who's writing to you from Italy?'

'You remember Alice?' said Thomas dreamily.

'Alice who?'

'*Our* Alice,' said Thomas still dreamily. He was remembering his fair-haired little sister – the one who was quite unlike the rest of the family, who loved books and music and pictures, and who had fallen in love with a foreign painter chap, a student at the art school, and run away to Italy with him.

'Of course I remember your Alice,' said Bessie. 'Sly, moony little thing!' (Her own private opinion of Thomas's

70

sister.) 'What about your Alice?'

'She's dead,' said Thomas. 'In fact she died more than two years ago, and there was me sending her Christmas cards, and never knew! She's left a child – a little girl.'

Bessie Waybridge's expression changed from mild interest (a death was always interesting) to deep suspicion.

'Thomas, you don't mean—'

He nodded.

'Poor little thing – there's nowhere else for her to go.'

'Where has she been all this time?' demanded Mrs. Waybridge. 'Tell me that! Somebody must have took her.' (In her agitation she was forgetting all her carefully acquired grammar). 'Well, that somebody can just go on looking after her. They didn't trouble to let us know at the time, so they've no call to come on us now.'

Silently Thomas handed her Father Bartolomeo's letter telling of Papa Angelino's death.

'It's monstrous!' exclaimed Bessie, when she had finished reading it. 'After two whole years to suddenly come on us. We can't take the child. We haven't the room.'

Monica, who had come in and was now reading the letter over her mother's shoulder, burst out: 'Well, she can't share *my* room, and that's flat! There's only room for *me* in it.' (Incidentally, Monica was voicing her philosophy of life – only room for *me!*)

'She can have the box-room,' said Thomas.

'And what about the suitcases, if I may ask?' demanded Bessie. '*And* the projector for the camera, and all your fishing things?'

'You can get rid of them,' said Thomas. 'I never have time to fish now, anyway.' He might have added: 'Too busy money-grubbing to keep *you* satisifed', but he didn't. He had no wish to upset the missis at such a crucial moment as this. 'I'll clear the place out with my own hands,' he added, 'and the money I get for my rods I'll put towards a new car. How will that do?'

71

But if he thought this would appease Bessie he was sadly mistaken.

'It's quite impossible,' she said, cutting a slice of bread for Cyril, who had just appeared.

'What's impossible?' demanded that young man. 'Tea, Mum, please – and get a move on, I'm late.'

'This idea of your father's that we should take into our home a penniless Italian brat,' said his mother. 'She's the kid of that sister of your father's – Alice her name was – who ran off to Italy with a painter.'

'It was all quite respectable,' broke in Thomas, 'and the "brat" is my niece, remember, and therefore yours. Anyway, the idea is not impossible because I telephoned a cable through before you were up this morning telling them to send her over to us straight away.'

The noise that broke out in the Waybridges' kitchen-dining-room at this startling announcement might have been compared to the Tower of Babel, except that it was all in one language! They all talked at once, but Mrs Waybridge's voice, being the most strident, came out on top. It was stopped short, however, by the clock striking half-past eight.

'Holy Moses!' exclaimed the son of the house. 'I must beat it! 'Bye, Mum!' He crammed a school cap on his handsome head and vanished, not waiting for his sister, who, having snatched up her school satchel, rushed after him, only to rush back a few minutes later.

'Forgot my dancing things!' she panted. 'There's a special rehearsal for that show on Tuesday, so I'll be late home. Keep my supper for me. 'Bye, Mum!'

The house was suddenly empty, for Thomas had slipped out too, having no wish to be left alone with his wife in her present state of mind.

'Italian brat!' thought Bessie. 'Huh!' Plenty to do to look after her own children. It was always Thomas's family who wanted helping. First there had been his brother George, who had borrowed money and hadn't repaid it (nor ever would); then there was his mother, who died penniless, and Thomas had insisted upon putting up a stone for her, and now *this* . . . The whine of the vacuum-cleaner echoed her feelings! She looked at the telephone receiver sitting so innocently on its hook, and felt it was rather like a pet dog who had turned on her and bitten her! If it hadn't been for that dratted cable . . . oh, well – there was nothing she could do about it now. Thomas didn't often make up his mind, but when he *did* she knew it was no use arguing with him. Stubborn as a mule, was Thomas!

Chapter 2

Cyril

Bessie Waybridge, like so many hard women, was anything but hard towards her own children – she spoilt them shamelessly. Whatever they asked for, they got – within reason, and often without reason. When Monica came home at the end of her first week at her new school and announced that, 'Everyone's got television in our form, Mum,' Bessie began looking at the hire-purchase adverts.

'Not everyone, surely?' she said mildly.

'Everyone who's anyone,' declared Monica (actually it was only one family). 'Oh, Mum, we simply *must* have the telly.' So the Waybridges acquired a television set, and if it was a bit of a strain keeping up the payments, still it was well worth it, thought Bessie, every time she came home from a shopping expedition and beheld the long inverted

'H' tacked on to the chimney of Hayfield Lodge. It made her feel so very superior to the people on either side!

It was the same with everything – the Waybridge children had but to ask and they received. Monica wanted dancing lessons ('Of course, my pet, and so you shall'), a nylon net *tutu* ('Monica must have what the other children have'), a full-length party frock ('Well, Thomas, the child's growing up'). Cyril wanted a ciné camera and a new bicycle (the old one hadn't got all the latest gadgets). They never even thought of thanking their parents when they got these things, nor did Bessie, at any rate, expect them to. They were *her* children – what more need be said?

Into this self-sufficient household came little Rosanna Corelli, used to the warmth, sunshine, poverty, and friendliness of southern Italy. What did she make of it? We can only guess her thoughts as she paused for the first time on the threshold of the Waybridges' resplendent lounge with its fitted carpet of a bright pink, its highly polished shoddy modern furniture, the settee heaped with plump pink satin cushions, with a matching chair, also much cushioned, at either side of the fireplace. In one corner stood the television set, and in another a fire-screen depicting the Coronation (worked in cross-stitch by Bessie). There were no original pictures (merely a set of gaudy flower-prints in colours chosen to match the room), no piano, no books. From between the layers of pink art silk curtains, and white net *brise-bise*, could be seen the house on the opposite side of the road – exactly the same, except that here the curtains were green. In the window opposite was a plaster statuette of a girl in high-heeled shoes doing some sort of a dance. These figurines were all the fashion in Denton Drive. Mrs Waybridge had gone one better than the house opposite by having *two* figures dancing a *pas de deux!*

Yes, Rosanna must have found life in Denton Drive strange, to put it mildly. After the friendly atmosphere of the steps and stairs of Amalfi, it must have seemed unusual that the Waybridges were not on speaking terms with the neighbours on either side. In the house joined on to their own lived a real working-class family, without pretensions. The children went to the council school and were 'very rough' (Bessie's words). Their father used to wander in and out of the house on Saturday mornings, unshaven, and in his shirt sleeves, tinkering with his car.

The family who lived on the other side were of the professional class. They were called Thompson, and Mr Thompson was a cashier in a bank. They hadn't a car, but their two children went to boarding school, and talked with la-de-da voices (said Bessie Waybridge, with envy). She knew, because she'd heard them talking through the hedge that separated 54 Denton Drive from Hayfield Lodge.

Those hedges! Rosanna looked out of her box-room window with amazement at the two neat rows of houses that composed Denton Drive, each cut off from its neighbour by a clipped hedge, or a rambler-rose-covered fence. Rosanna had no idea at all about 'keeping herself to herself' or 'minding her own business', said Bessie to her husband a week after the child's arrival.

'I caught her yesterday talking to that awful Higginbottom man about the tomatoes in his beastly little greenhouse, and today there she was, as bold as brass, talking over the fence to Mrs Thompson about the roses.'

'Oh, well,' said Thomas (who privately would have liked very much to fraternise with 'that awful Higginbottom man'), 'she doesn't know any better. You must make allowances for her, my dear.'

'She'll have to get it into her head that it just isn't done to gossip with the neighbours,' said Bessie. 'Why, we might just as well be living on a council estate where everyone spends half the day gossiping over the fence!'

Although lots of Rosanna's little ways (such as leaving her meat untouched at the side of her plate and living on vegetables and fruit) irritated Bessie, to do her justice she was not actively hostile to the child. As a matter of fact she didn't see a great deal of her. Rosanna went to school (the council school down the road) at eight-thirty in the morning, stayed there for midday dinner, and returned home at four o'clock. At first she used to go up to her bedroom (which was still full of boxes and suitcases that Thomas, with the best will in the world, hadn't been able to find a place for elsewhere) and sit there, thinking about her home, and Anya, and her precious dancing lessons. These took on a dreamlike quality, as if they had happened to someone else, or in another life, so that she had to think very hard to make herself believe they had really happened to *her*. Then, when the weather grew darker and colder, and Christmas drew near, she was driven from her refuge to seek the warmth below. Usually she sat by herself in the kitchen, not daring to join the family gathered round a roaring fire in the lounge enjoying the telly. She still wore her thin cotton frocks that she had brought from Italy, but Bessie had found one or two of Monica's old jumpers (that hadn't been sent to the parish jumble sale) and an outgrown coat, but even then Rosanna was never really warm. For one thing, she had caught a cold. Colds were almost unknown in the south of Italy, and in consequence she had built up no resistance to them. Most of her schoolmates had colds and snivelled, but Rosanna was really ill. If Cyril or Monica had come down to breakfast with faces as pale and wan as Rosanna's Bessie would have sent for the doctor, but since it was just Rosanna she didn't bother. 'Making a fuss about nothing!' she said brightly. 'You'll just have to make the best of it, Rosanna. Everyone in England catches a cold now and then.'

So, taking it all round, Rosanna was as miserable a small girl as you would find anywhere. To add to her troubles, along came Cyril to torment her. Up to now he'd been far too occupied with his own affairs to bother his handsome head about his small cousin, but then one cold Saturday morning, at the beginning of December (when snow had stopped sport), he had a mind to tease her.

'Come here, brat!' he ordered, seeing her crouched beside the kitchen stove as usual. Then, as she didn't appear to understand, he repeated: 'Come here, you, when you're told. Didn't you hear what I said?'

'*Si – si –* ' said Rosanna, her English forsaking her in her terror. What was this boy – this awful boy – going to do to her?

'Don't "*si*" me!' exclaimed Cyril. 'You've lived in England long enough to say "yes", haven't you?'

'*Si* – I mean yes,' whispered Rosanna.

'From now on, you're going to be my fag,' announced Cyril. 'Fag – F-A-G. Does that mean anything to you, brat?' Rosanna shook her head.

'It will,' said Cyril smoothly. 'May I explain. When I want anything, I shout for it and *you* run and get it. Understand? That's the English public-school fag system that you've no doubt heard about. If you don't run fast enough, you get beaten.' He picked up the toasting-fork and made swishing noises with it. He wasn't in earnest, but poor Rosanna didn't know it. She was filled with terror.

'I'll show you how it works,' went on Cyril. '*Camera . . .* Go on, find it! It will probably be hanging on a hook on the hall-stand. Run!'

Rosanna ran, found the camera, and brought it to him obediently.

The rest of the morning was a nightmare. Cyril spent it shouting the names of his possessions at regular intervals, and Rosanna running for them all over the house and garden. But at midday something happened that altered things for Rosanna. By the afternoon post came a letter with an Italian stamp. It was addressed to Signorina Rosanna Francesca Corelli in big sprawling handwriting, and the postmark was that of Amalfi.

77

' "Here's a thing and a very pretty thing",' sang Cyril when he saw it lying on the door mat. 'What must I do with this pretty thing?' He picked it up and carried it into the lounge. 'Rosanna!' he yelled, and when she appeared he waved the letter over his head. 'Here's a letter for you from Italy, brat.'

'Oh, give it to me, please,' she begged, a flush of delight coming into her pale cheeks.

'Not so fast, my lady!' said Cyril, brandishing the letter aloft. 'First you must fetch me my – let me see – my football boots. You'll find them, I think, in the garage.'

But Rosanna hadn't moved.

'Go on, brat!' ordered Cyril. 'Run! Otherwise!' He made a movement of throwing the letter into the fire.

Rosanna's Italian temper (damped down up to now by the cold and her own misery) flared.

'Give it to me!' she cried, and sprang at him in a fury, shouting Italian epithets, and striking him with her fists.

'She was like a blinking wild cat,' said Cyril afterwards to Monica. 'Attacked me tooth and nail – literally, I can tell you! I bear the marks! It was all I could do to keep her at bay. She got her letter all right – cheap at the price! Gosh, what a virago!'

'What's a virago?' asked Monica with interest.

'A wild woman,' said Cyril. 'And come to think of it, I have a notion it's an Italian word. What a joke!'

Upstairs, crouched on her bed, Rosanna was reading her letter. It was from Anya, telling her all the news of her home – how a film company had visited the town, and a lot of local people had been called in as 'extras' (and had been paid too!). One of her pupils – Marianna Vittorini – had got a real part in the film as a dancer. Another of her pupils had joined the Marquis de Cuevas ballet company, and was now at Monte Carlo dancing in the Opera House; another was coming to England in the autumn to train at the Sadler's Wells school. A famous novelist had come to live in a villa near her own, and was busy writing a book about Amalfi.

At the end of the letter came news that made Rosanna's eyes shine for the first time since she had come to live in the cold grey north of England.

'One day last week,' wrote Anya, 'I had a visit from a handsome young man. He told me his name was Giorgio Cantoni, and that you had both lived with an uncle of his until the old man died. I gathered his uncle was the "Papa Angelino" you talked to me about. Well, Giorgio has started work for a fisherman, and is sure that, one day, he'll have a boat of his own. He asked me for your address, and said I was to tell you he would be writing to you himself, and that he would never forget you. Besides being handsome, he seemed to me to be a dear boy.

Well, Rosanna, I will stop now. Do not forget what I told you the night you left me – your dancing must always come first.

All my love,
Your friend,
Anya Boccaccio.'

Rosanna cried when she read the letter, but her tears were tears of happiness. She was not forgotten after all. She could write to Anya, and to Giorgio too, for before very long she would know his address.

That night she slept dreamlessly, almost for the first time since her arrival in England. Night after night her sleep had been haunted by nightmares of people who chased her down the tunnelled alleyways of Amalfi, trying to catch her and to imprison her away from the sunlight. Her outburst had done some good, moreover. Cyril never openly tormented her again, though he never forgot the way she had attacked him. He bided his time. One day he would pay her back!

Chapter 3

Monica

Monica's teasing took a more subtle form than her brother's. She began by showing an interest in Rosanna's life in Italy, and then, when Rosanna eagerly answered her questions, poking fun at her.

'Where did you live in Amalfi?' she asked one day. 'Was it a house like this?'

Rosanna looked round the modern lounge of Hayfield Lodge (soft chairs, plump satin cushions, television set, but no music, books, or beautiful pictures) and in her mind's eye beheld Papa Angelino's home in the old tenement house at the top of the long flights of stairs – the luminous green-tiled floor, the ancient corner-cupboard, the ceiling with its cupids and its clouds, the picture of the blue-robed, sad-eyed Madonna shining out of the dimness of the living-room. She remembered the flat roof ablaze with sunlight, and in her imagination saw the picturesque huddled houses of Amalfi lying below like a bunch of bright flowers, and heard the bells in all the little campaniles chiming the lazy hours. A wave of homesickness engulfed her (which was possibly what Monica intended). She shook her head. No, her home had not been like Hayfield Lodge.

'I suppose you hadn't a bathroom?' persisted Monica.

Again Rosanna shook her head, remembering the marble trough at the bottom of the crumbling steps, and the winged bull that presided over it.

'Did you *never* have a bath then?'

'No – we bathed in the sea,' said Rosanna.

'Oh!' Monica was a little taken aback, but not for long. 'What about the winter?' she demanded. 'I suppose from October until June you never washed at all?'

'Oh, but in Amalfi it is warm long before June,' answered Rosanna. 'In March it is quite warm enough to bathe in the sea, and in November too.'

Monica abandoned the washing arrangements in Italy, and began to catechise Rosanna about her friends.

'I suppose you had lots of friends when you lived in Amalfi?' she said. 'What were their names?'

Rosanna considered the matter.

'Well – there was Giovanna—'

Monica burst into a brittle tinkle of laughter.

'Gee-o-varna! Gio-o-varna!' she mimicked. 'What a funny name!'

'Then there was Brigida, and Maria, and Giulia and Lola. They were my school-friends.'

'Didn't you have any *boys* at your school?' persisted Monica. 'Hadn't you any boy-friends?' She herself had plenty of these at her coeducational school. In a dark, hard way she was very pretty.

Rosanna shook her head. A picture came into her mind of Giorgio, with his bare brown feet, his black curls, and his passion for fishing, but something stopped her from telling Monica about Giorgio. A few days ago a letter had come for her from Giorgio, but as the Waybridges had all been out when it had arrived, no one had seen it. It was only a few lines scrawled on a bit of paper torn off a cheap pad (Giorgio's strong suit was not letter writing!), but he had sent her a snapshot of himself (taken by Anya, so he said) with his best love. She had hidden the photograph and the letter beneath Monica's outgrown jumper, next to her heart. It remained her secret.

'No, I hadn't any boy-friends,' she said.

Monica shrugged her shoulders, as much as to say, 'What could you expect of an Italian brat?'

Up to now there had been no actual outbreak of hostility between Rosanna and Monica, but one day just before Christmas Rosanna went upstairs to find the door of her bedroom open. This was nothing out of the ordinary, since, as we have said, the room still acted as the family junk-hole, and housed the Waybridges' suitcases, boxes and odds and ends. But on this occasion the curtain, which Thomas had put up in lieu of a wardrobe, had been pulled aside, displaying Rosanna's collection of washed-out print dresses, her one threadbare coat, and a couple of pairs of ancient shoes below.

Frantically Rosanna began to rummage amongst her belongings, looking for something that had disappeared – something exceedingly precious to her. She tore out of the boxroom, intending to find her aunt, and in doing so she passed Monica's room, the door of which was ajar. Through the opening she could just see Monica in her petticoat standing in front of the full-length mirror in her wardrobe, holding in front of her a beautiful white lace dress – the dress that had been given to Rosanna by her mysterious friend Leo, and which was her most cherished possession.

'Give that to me!' shouted Rosanna, rushing into the room with scant ceremony.

Monica, taken unawares with the frock half over her head, jumped guiltily, then recovered herself.

'Oh, Rosanna! You did give me a shock! I was just trying on your frock to see if it suited me.'

'Give it to me!' repeated Rosanna. 'How dare you try on my clothes!'

'My dear kid, I wouldn't try on your rags and tatters for a king's ransom,' declared Monica, 'but this frock is different. Where did you get it?'

'It was given to me – by a friend,' answered Rosanna.

'And I see you've got all the things to wear underneath as well,' went on Monica, and then Rosanna saw that the beautiful underclothes she had worn beneath the frock for the ballet at Covent Garden were all spread out on Monica's bed.

'It's nothing to do with you what I wear,' said Rosanna.

82

'All those things were given to me, and they're *mine*.'

'I'm not so sure about that,' argued Monica. 'My mum and dad have to keep you and buy your clothes, so by rights these things ought to be sold to help pay for your food.'

Like Cyril she was half-joking, but there was a lot of truth in her words. Rosanna *was* totally dependent upon her relations for every bite she ate, and every stitch of clothing she wore (even if it was Monica's cast-off jumper).

'You shan't have them! You shan't have them!' she cried, the tears rolling down her cheeks. She picked up the frock which Monica had dropped upon the floor, gathered up the filmy undergarments, pushed them back into the box with trembling hands, and took them to her own room. She shut the door, and looked round for a hiding-place. Finally she turned down her bedclothes, and pushed the dress and everything that went with it between the mattress and the calico cover that had been put on to protect it. The precious dress would be crushed, but it would be safe. They would never think of looking for it here!

Monica didn't tell her mother about the affair. Like Cyril, she kept the matter to herself, thinking that the knowledge might be useful some day. As a matter of fact Bessie Waybridge knew all about the lace dress and the other things. She had noted the large box that Rosanna had carried so carefully on the day of her arrival, and, curiosity getting the better of her, had looked inside. Rosanna was only a child, she argued, and ought to have no secrets from those who were taking care of her. She did not (unlike Monica) realise the value of the clothes, but she had a vague feeling that they might come in handy – for Monica's dancing perhaps, or for a fancy dress costume for Monica's school play. Rosanna, being wholly dependent upon her kind relations, could hardly refuse to lend them.

Chapter 4 ·

Rosanna tries to make Money

Rosanna got on quite well at the council school down the road. At first the other children had been inclined to laugh at her foreign accent, but they soon got used to her, and accepted her as one of themselves. She found some of the lessons difficult, especially arithmetic, but her English progressed by leaps and bounds, and she was soon chattering away to her schoolmates with a Tyneside accent you could cut with a knife!

'Ha-way, man!' shouted little Rosanna Corelli, much to Bessie's disgust. Oh, well, she thought, it wasn't as if Rosanna were her own child. Thank goodness both Cyril and Monica were well-spoken!

Christmas came and went, with expensive presents for the Waybridge children, and cheap ones for Rosanna. Not that she minded – Rosanna's tastes were simple in the extreme. From Italy there came a pair of real Italian ballet shoes (Anya had remembered her size, and chosen a size larger to allow for six months' growth), and a lace handkerchief from Giorgio. With these gifts Rosanna was content. She wouldn't have changed them for Monica's wristwatch, nor Cyril's record-player.

The ballet shoes (which she had not as yet shown to the family) prompted her to screw up her courage and ask her aunt if she could have some dancing lessons. Monica, she knew, learnt at Mary Martin's, and this was the teacher Anya Boccaccio had talked to her about.

'Dancing lessons?' echoed Bessie, wondering if she had heard right. The cheek of the kid! Who did she think she was? Weren't she and Thomas doing enough for her – feeding and clothing her? 'No, of course you can't have dancing lessons. Whatever gave you such an idea?'

'Monica—' murmured Rosanna.

'That is *quite* different,' snapped Bessie. 'Monica is our own daughter, and very talented. She'll go on the stage, and become a great star like Margot Fonteyn. Her dancing is part of her education. It's quite different with you, Rosanna. You will have your living to make, so you must work hard and learn enough English for you to become a shorthand-typist, or perhaps a nurse. We'll see later on. Meanwhile it's very good of your uncle to take you in, and pay for your food and clothes. He couldn't possibly afford to give you luxuries such as dancing lessons. It's quite out of the question, so let us hear no more of it.'

'No, Aunt Bessie,' said Rosanna obediently. Then, just as her aunt was going out of the kitchen, she added: 'It's just the money, isn't it? I mean, if I had enough money—'

' "If ifs and ands were pots and pans" ' quoted Bessie. 'You *haven't* the money, Rosanna, so the matter is settled.'

But the matter wasn't settled – not in Rosanna's mind. All during the Christmas holidays she thought about money, and how she could get some. It had been easy in Italy. You just danced, and people gave you money – lots of it! Why not here, in England? Once she had been sent into town to collect a parcel from a special quick-service dry-cleaner, and on her way home she had seen a long procession of people queueing for the gallery outside one of the main theatres. It gave her an idea. She would dance for the queue, and collect enough money for a term's dancing lessons.

And so one Saturday in early January, about a week before the new school term, Rosanna spent part of the morning looking out something to dance in. Ah, there it was at the bottom of the box in which she kept her under-clothes – a skirt of red sateen, trimmed with rows of black braid, and a little bolero to match. She had worn them when she had danced at the Hotel Santa Lucia. She packed

them into her school satchel, along with her cherished castanets, and set off for Newcastle. Nobody saw her go except
Cyril, who was in the garage mending a puncture in his
bicycle tyre. He left the tyre and followed her. There was
a purposeful air about her – as if she were setting out on a
special mission, and Cyril determined to find out what it
was. Not for nothing had his nose a long inquisitive point
at the end! When Rosanna boarded the bus, and climbed
up to the top deck, Cyril stepped on too, but stayed down
below. When Rosanna alighted at Grey's Monument, Cyril
swung off also, though he was careful to remain unseen.

There was a cup-tie match being played at St James's Park
that particular Saturday afternoon, and most of the police
were at the other end of the town, so Rosanna had a field
day! For the best part of an hour she amused the matinée
theatre queue with her gipsy dancing, accompanying herself
with her castanets. She collected so many copper and silver
coins in her beret that she had to stop and empty it into
her pocket half way, and start again. Never had the crowd
seen anything they liked better. When the gallery doors
opened, they were quite reluctant to go inside! And all
the time Cyril Waybridge watched tirelessly from a nearby
doorway. When the last of the queue had vanished into the
theatre and Rosanna turned to go, out he came and grasped
her by the arm.

'What do you mean by bringing your disreputable Italian
ways here and begging in the streets?' he demanded. 'Don't
you know that in England it's considered shameful to beg
for money?'

'Oh, it's you, Cyril!' exclaimed Rosanna. 'What a fright
you gave me! I didn't mean no harm.'

'*Any* harm,' corrected Cyril. 'Well, if you didn't know
before that begging is shameful, you know now. Come with
me.' Still grasping her arm firmly he propelled her across
the road to another street, on the corner of which stood

one of those old city churches which have, through no fault of their own, lost their congregations, owing to warehouses, shops, and offices having replaced dwelling houses. It was very dark inside, and on a small table at the foot of the aisle stood an ancient carved box with a slit in the top. Propped against it was a printed notice saying: THE CHURCH OF ENGLAND SOCIETY FOR DESTITUTE ORPHAN CHILDREN, and underneath, written in pencil: 'Please give generously.'

'Now!' said Cyril, leading Rosanna up to it. 'You can put all your ill-gotten gains in there,' and he pointed to the box. He didn't lower his voice, nor bow to the altar, but stood over the girl aggressively.

'*Santa Maria!*' whispered Rosanna, curtsying deeply and crossing herself as she had been taught to do by the Italian priests.

'Go on,' repeated Cyril. 'You heard what I said.'

'You mean I must put it in the box – all of it?'

'Yes, all of it – every penny,' said Cyril. (He'd teach her to attack him – biting and scratching!)

With her heart breaking Rosanna obeyed. She could hardly do otherwise with Cyril's grasp tightening on her arm. He was quite twice as big as she was and a great deal stronger.

'And now we shall see what you have got in your pocket,' said the boy when she had emptied the beret. 'Ah, I thought so! Quite a pile! Be quick and put it in. Can't wait here all day. St Christopher's is going to wonder where all this lot came from!'

When the last penny had disappeared into the slit, Cyril released the girl's arm.

'Well, now I'll be off. So glad I was on hand to help you with your good deed. See you this evening.' He turned and left her, and Rosanna heard him whistling as he strode away up the street.

She wandered up to the altar. It was bitterly cold in the

dim church, and silent as the tomb. Not much traffic came down this street (especially on Saturday, when the shops were shut), and the little there was was deadened by the double set of baize doors leading from the porch. Above the altar were three pointed stained-glass windows depicting with horrible realism scenes from the Crucifixion. Rosanna turned away from them to a smaller window in the chancel. It was of very old, rich, dark, stained glass, and there was a figure of Christ (many times larger than life) with a crowd of children gathered round His knees. Some of them were sitting on His lap, and one was peeping over His shoulder. It was a beautiful, comforting picture – the face of Christ infinitely gentle, and full of compassion.

Rosanna had always prayed to the Holy Virgin, but there was no Holy Mother here, so she prayed to Jesus instead.

'Oh, sir,' she said under her breath. 'Please, *please* help me! I'm sorry if it was wrong to beg, but I didn't mean no – I should say any harm. It's only that I want my dancing lessons so very badly. Please tell me how to get some.'

She looked round for a candle to light, but there were none in this church. Evidently one didn't have to pay for one's prayers, but maybe they got answered just the same. She wondered why she had not thought about praying for her dancing lessons before. She left the church with perfect faith that somehow, sometime, her prayer would be answered.

Chapter 5

The Free Class

When Rosanna went back to school she found the other place at her double desk filled by an olive-skinned little girl with hair and eyes as dark as her own.

'My name's Laura Montessori,' she said. 'What's yours?'

When Rosanna told her, of course they exchanged life stories and it appeared that, although Laura had an Italian name, and was obviously of Italian parentage, she had never been to Italy. Her grandparents had come from a small Italian village to England and had started an ice-cream business in Newcastle. Their son (Laura's father) had married an Italian girl who had lived in England all her life, and they had carried on the business. When Laura was three years old they had moved to Hayfield, which was just beginning to grow up, and which offered greater opportunities for trade than the town in which people no longer lived, but only came to shop. And this was how Laura had come to attend the Hayfield Council School. The fact that Rosanna hadn't seen her before was because she had been in hospital during the last weeks of the autumn term.

The teacher of the class had put Rosanna and Laura at the same desk because, as she said to the head teacher, she was 'sorry for that poor little Rosanna Corelli – having to live with those Waybridges. I still remember the two Waybridge children – what were their names? Oh, yes, Monica and Cyril – clever, I grant you, but not the sympathetic type. Now there's something about Rosanna that catches at your heart . . .'

Rosanna's friendship with the Montessoris altered her whole life. They had a shop where ice-cream (such as only Italians know how to make) and cigarettes and chocolates

89

were sold. The shop was never shut because, although the blind would be drawn down ostentatiously on Sundays and holidays and at six o'clock on weekdays, everybody knew you had only to go round to the back, and Elena would sell you whatever you wanted.

The Montessoris lived in the big room behind the shop, and by the looks of it they slept there too! It was always warm, comfortable, and untidy, no matter what time of the day you went there. Although the house was a typical English bungalow, it had acquired an Italian flavour. There was a huge black stove that puffed out waves of heat, and curtains of brightly coloured bamboo shut off the living-room from the shop and from the other rooms. Rosanna had never seen the other rooms, nor had she seen any of the Montessoris enter them. They remained as mysterious as Bluebeard's chamber! To add to the Italian flavour, the Montessoris had altered the name of the bungalow from Rose Cottage to Villa Rosita. It was so warm in the Montessoris' living-room that Rosanna got really thawed out for the first time since she had arrived in England. She used to dance for them, and tell them about the Italy they had never seen (but talked of retiring to), and they grew to love her dearly. Elena would gather Rosanna to her, and murmur extravagant Italian endearments (learned from her mother who *had* lived in Italy) over the child.

Elena was a huge woman with jet-black hair and eyes like dark brown velvet, and a large generous mouth that opened wide to show two rows of magnificent white teeth. When she laughed (which was often) she shook like a jelly, and almost rocked the jerry-built bungalow. Laura, on the other hand, was small and thin, with hair parted demurely down the centre, and luminous dark eyes, sometimes sad, but mostly shining with mischief. (Incidentally she spoke with a broad Tyneside accent!) Antonio Montessori had tight black curls and very white teeth under a Charlie Chaplin moustache. He went round Hayfield with his ice-cream cart singing 'Santa Lucia', and 'Funiculi Funicula' in a beautiful melodious voice, and one felt that, had he not been an ice-cream vendor, he would have made a splendid operatic tenor.

Bessie did not know about Rosanna's friendship with the Montessoris. Rosanna did not tell her about them, feeling instinctively that she would not approve of them – especially the living-room! When she was asked to the Montessoris for tea, she just asked if she might go to 'a school friend's', and Bessie was only too glad to get rid of her and not interested enough to ask who the friend was.

One day in the middle of February Bessie, encouraged by a few watery gleams of sunshine, had decided to start the spring cleaning. She had begun on Monica's bedroom, so as to 'work downwards' in the proper way. By five o'clock she had got to the stage of putting up the newly washed curtains when the telephone rang. She was about to shout down the stairs for Rosanna to answer it when she remembered that Rosanna could never understand people's voices on the 'phone, so decided to attend to it herself. Rosanna, sitting in the kitchen eating her tea (she had got used to the English fashion of tea by now) and polishing Monica's brass fender at the same time, heard her aunt stump down the stairs, which had been stripped of their stair-carpets for the spring cleaning, and go into the lounge. In a few minutes she was at the kitchen door.

'That was Monica,' she said. 'She's at her dancing school. There's an important class this evening – Royal Academy of Dancing – and someone very important from Sadler's Wells School is taking it. The child has forgotten the belt of her dance-tunic – she washed and ironed it yesterday, and I suppose she forgot to put the belt on again.' (The truth was that *Rosanna* had washed and ironed it, but Monica, in her headlong rush to school in the morning, had left the belt hanging on the airer.) 'You'd better leave that,' went on Mrs Waybridge, indicating the fender, 'and take it along to her. She says it's *most* important, and she can't possibly dance without it. You can have your tea when you come back. Here's your bus fare – you get off at the corner of Rothbury Crescent.' She wasn't thinking about Rosanna's legs, but the quickest way to get the belt to Monica.

When Rosanna arrived at the Mary Martin School of Dancing she found the class on the point of starting. Monica saw her from a window, and dashed down to meet her on the stairs. She didn't thank Rosanna, but snatched the belt with a hurried, 'I thought you'd *never* come! You're only just in time. Don't forget to shut the door – Mary hates it left open.' She disappeared, along with a crowd of other students, into the big studio.

Rosanna went down the stairs, and dutifully shut the outer door, which had been open when she came, but she didn't go away. She crept back up the staircase, and stood listening at the studio door. She could hear people talking, and then a ripple of music. It was the same music that she had danced to many a time in Anya's studio. On the far side of the landing was a small practice room, with a *barre* and a mirror. It was quite empty, of course, since all the students were in the big studio. Rosanna hesitated. Would anyone mind if she did just a few exercises? In any case, nobody would know.

She kicked off her shoes, threw her coat down upon the floor, for there were no chairs, and began to practise *pliés*. Then on to *battements sur le coup de pied*. Then centre practice. All the time she could hear the music, faintly but clearly, from the big studio. She could almost (but not quite) hear the words of command of the teacher.

Mary Martin, coming out of the class to seek a register, paused on the threshold of the practice room, and beheld an astonishing sight. An extraordinarily beautiful and graceful little girl was dancing exquisitely all by herself in the empty room! Moreover she was dancing with all her heart and soul. Jealousy filled Mary's heart. Which ballet school owned this lovely child? Which school (and she knew them all) could possibly have trained a dancer like this? The child's *portes de bras* were big and flowing, her beautifully turned out limbs, her strongly arched feet, the graceful carriage of her head, set on a long slender neck, her expressive face, her whole style – oh, it was just not possible! Mary couldn't bear to think that the child hadn't been trained by *her*! Or that someone else would take the credit for giving this dancer to the world.

And then suddenly a thought struck her – up to now she had been far too astonished to think clearly. Why was this child here, dressed in her everyday clothes, with bare feet, instead of in the big studio? She coughed, and Rosanna nearly fell to the ground. She had come back all the way from Anya's studio in Italy to this bare little room, and now she must explain herself to this strange woman, who, though she had a kind face, had every right to be angry.

'I – I'm sorry,' she stammered, the rapt expression on her face changed now to unhappiness. 'I wasn't doing no – I mean *any* harm.'

'No, of course you weren't, dear,' said Mary Martin. 'But why aren't you in class? Were you too late? Of course it was very naughty of you not to be here earlier, but still I think we can let you in just this once. You'll be in time for the *enchainements*, if you're very quick. Run along, dear, and change.'

'Change?' echoed Rosanna, her eyes wide. 'But I'm not a student here.'

'No, of course I know that,' said Mary, beginning to be irritated. (Surely this child, who danced so deliciously, wasn't a half-wit? That would be too awful!) 'I know all my own students, naturally. I suppose you come from one of the visiting schools. Several of them have sent pupils to this R.A.D. free class. Which one do you belong to, dear?'

'I don't belong to any school,' said Rosanna.

Mary's brow puckered. She began to think it was *she* who was the half-wit!

'Then what were you doing here?' she asked.

'I came with Monica's belt.'

'Monica? Monica who?' (There were several Monicas in the school.)

'Monica Waybridge, my cousin. And then, when I gave it to her, I heard the music, and I just *had* to dance. You see I haven't danced since I left Italy.' Rosanna's eyes became bright at the thought of it. 'You don't mind – I wasn't doing no – any – harm.'

Mary Martin made one of her usual, swift, decisions.

'Would you like to join in the class?' she asked.

Rosanna's eyes shone, not with tears now, but joy. Then her face fell.

'Oh, but I haven't got a dance tunic,' she said.

Mary took her by the arm.

'Come in here,' she said, and led the way to the dressing-room. It was full of the students' clothes lying in heaps on the benches and hanging on the pegs. Shoes, attaché cases, bags, and parcels lay all over the floor. Stepping across them, rather as if they were stepping-stones, Mary crossed to a large wardrobe, took down from the top a cardboard box, and withdrew a number of black ballet tunics, and several pairs of ballet shoes.

'Take this one, and these,' she said, handing a tunic and a pair of shoes to the astonished Rosanna. 'I think they will fit. If not, there are plenty of others in here for you to choose from. I keep them for emergencies. When you have changed, wait outside the studio door until I go in, then creep in behind me and take your place in the back row. Mr Delahaye will never notice. Be quick, now, or it won't be worth your going in.'

*

After the class was over Mary Martin called Rosanna into her room.

'Tell me, dear,' she said, 'where did you learn to dance so beautifully? You did dance beautifully, you know – Mr Delahaye noticed you particularly.'

'I learned from Madame Boccaccio,' said Rosanna, blushing with happiness. She was all warm and glowing now after the hard class, and you would hardly have recognised in her the sad-faced, half-frozen little girl who had crept into the practice room a short hour before.

'Anya Boccaccio?' said Mary Martin aloud, then added, half to herself, 'I thought so! I thought the child must be the pupil of some great dancer. Ballet is such an aristocratic art. How very strange! Then this child does not belong to any of the local schools. In that case she must certainly belong to *mine* . . . You're Monica Waybridge's cousin, I think you said?' she added, turning back to Rosanna. 'Will your aunt let you train with me, do you think?'

Rosanna shook her head.

'I asked her, but she wouldn't.'

'Why not, my dear?' asked Mary Martin gently. She couldn't understand anyone not recognising talent and fostering it.

'She said they were a luxury,' said Rosanna. 'Dancing classes, I mean.'

'Well, so they are in many cases,' agreed Mary. 'But in your case they might be an investment. You might take up dancing professionally. Have you thought about that? I'll call and have a word with your aunt about it.'

'It won't be no – any use,' said Rosanna sadly. 'She says I've got to be a shorthand-typist.'

'We'll see, we'll see,' said Mary soothingly. 'Run along now, dear. I'll be round to see your aunt. You can depend upon me.'

'It won't be no use,' said Rosanna desperately to herself as she left the school. 'They pays for my food and clothes, but there's no money for dancing lessons.'

Meanwhile Monica had run home with such a tale to tell. Rosanna had arrived at Mary's with her belt, and had somehow pushed herself into the R.A.D. class.

'Yes, in a tunic and proper shoes and everything! I don't know where she got them. And d'you know, Mum, Mr Delahaye, though he tried to hide it, never took his eyes off her. Looked at her all the time out of the corner of his eye, and hadn't as much as a glance to spare for *me*. And Mary too! Kept her back after the class and talked to her in her private room . . . Yes, of course I listened at the door, but I couldn't hear what they said. It's my belief they were hatching something.'

'The slyness of it!' exclaimed her mother. 'You'd hardly believe it – such a meek, whey-faced little thing!'

Chapter 6

The Lace Dress

After her talk with Mary Martin (stiffened by Anya's letter urging her to 'put her dancing first') Rosanna began to think again about making money. She mentioned the matter to the Montessoris when she went there to tea the next day.

'Isn't there *anything* I can do to make money?' she said despairingly. 'In Italy I could have danced and collected enough for a term's dancing lessons in no time, but here—'

'No, in England it is not so easy,' said Elena Montessori. 'Haven't you anything – say jewellery – you could sell?

There's a "pop" round the corner.' (She meant a pawnbroker.)

Rosanna shook her head.

'Only this necklace.' She put her hand up to her throat where sparkled a beautiful Venetian glass necklace. 'My father gave it to me. It's the only thing I have to remember him by. I *couldn't* part with my necklace.'

'Yes, it would be hard,' agreed Elena. 'Well, we must think of something else. Of course you haven't any *clothes*' – she regarded Rosanna's old print frock not very hopefully – 'and in any case,' she added sadly, 'they do not give you a great deal for them. I sold an old fur coat and all I got was a few pounds.'

But Rosanna's face had lighted up.

'Oh, Elena, darling Elena, I *have* some clothes. They're my very dearest possession (next to my necklace), but I'd sell them all for my dancing lessons.' Rosanna, you see, was growing up. She realised now that the lace dress, lovely though it was, could be replaced, but the necklace chosen especially for her by her dead father could not. 'I'll bring my lovely clothes to show you,' she cried in excitement.

She danced away from the Villa Rosita so lightly that her feet scarcely touched the ground. Her dancing lessons seemed to have come very near. Surely, surely the lace dress and all the other things would pay for them. When she reached the corner of Denton Drive she sobered down, and became once more her quiet, sad-faced self. It wouldn't do if her aunt suspected anything. She must pack up the clothes in secret, and no one must see her when she left the house with them. There had been no slyness in Rosanna's nature when she had first come to Hayfield Lodge, but she was fast learning to be secretive.

Fortunately when she reached the house it was empty. Monica was at a rehearsal of the school play, Mrs Way-bridge at one of her meetings, Cyril out on his new bicycle. The coast was clear! Rosanna ran swiftly up to her little bedroom, and drawing aside the curtain looked for her cardboard box – the one in which she had kept the lace dress – she must pack the clothes in it. But it was not there! Someone had been in the closet looking for the dress – she was sure of it! She ran to her bed, and pulling down the bedclothes, felt inside the mattress. Yes, it was still there, and so were all the other things – even the silver shoes that made a lump where her feet came to. Thank goodness for such a good hiding-place!

She pulled out the clothes and packed as many of them as she could get into her school satchel. The rest she made up into a large brown-paper parcel, and tied it round with string. As she let herself out of the back door, she heard her aunt come in at the front. It was a near squeak!

When Elena saw the clothes she looked at Rosanna in amazement. Never had she imagined the child possessed anything like the beautiful garments spread out all over the Montessoris' living-room!

'Why, they're worth quite a lot of money,' she exclaimed, holding up the velvet party cloak, lined with white satin (padded underneath with cotton wool to make it warm). 'We'll go straight along to the shop and see what can be done. No, wait! First we must iron the things. They are so very crushed. They'll look a lot better after they have been pressed. Laura, switch on the iron!'

The whole Montessori family (including Antonio) helped with the ironing of the fairylike garments that were going to buy dancing lessons for their little friend. It was very romantic, when you came to think about it, but they didn't think – they were too intent upon their work. Laura held up the lace, so that it shouldn't fall upon the floor and get dirty, Rosanna damped the white cloth to go over the top, so that the delicate fabric shouldn't get scorched or damaged, and Elena wielded the iron. Antonio deftly folded the underclothes and put them into a box, murmuring Italian expressions of admiration as he did so. Oh, the warmth and friendliness of that Montessori living-room – warmth that came not only from the great iron stove, but from their hearts!

'And now for "Uncle's",' said Elena when they had finished. 'I'll carry the dress round in my arms, so as not to crush it again. Ah, but it is beautiful!'

'I didn't know he was your uncle,' said Rosanna innocently.

'No more he is, Rosanna *mia*,' said Elena, shaking all over with laughter. 'That's what they call the pawnbroker in England!'

'Uncle' turned out to be a dark-skinned little man, with a pronounced foreign accent. He was quick to see the value of the clothes – especially the filmy underclothes, all marked with the name of the famous London shop where they had been bought – but he was careful not to show it.

'Of course the party cloak,' he shrugged his shoulders expressively. 'There is no demand for such things here. The dress? Well, as you say it is nice, yes. I give you ten pound for them both. The shoes and the stockings – five pounds. The underclothes' (he turned them over carefully) 'I give you five pound for the lot. I pay you good, since I know the Momma' – he bowed to Elena – 'since a long time.'

'Very well,' said Elena. 'Twenty pounds it is'. Suddenly, on an impulse Rosanna ran round the counter and flung her arms round the little man much to his amazement.

'Thank you, thank you, Uncle!' she cried. 'You don't know what you've done for me!'

Back at the Villa Rosita, Elena produced an envelope and they put the money into it.

'You go straight along to Miss Martin's and give it to her,' she said. 'Don't you go taking it home. You don't want to lose it now you've got it!' (Elena, as can be seen, had no very great opinion of the Waybridges, possibly from what she had gathered from Rosanna.)

So Rosanna went off clutching the envelope with the money inside and Mary's name written on the back, but when she arrived at the dancing school the outer door was shut, and it was all too obvious that Mary was not in. So all she could do was to drop it in the letterbox. As a matter of fact, Mary (who lived in a flat above the studio) had gone round to see Mrs Waybridge about Rosanna, and was at this very moment sitting in the lounge of Hayfield Lodge talking to Bessie.

Being the soul of diplomacy, Mary talked first about Monica, the splendid progress she had made, and of how there was a good chance of her winning an R.A.D. scholarship, provided she worked hard, and didn't grow too big.

'I'm always haunted by that bogey!' she laughed. 'The fear that my pupils will grow too big.' Then, with deceptive nonchalance she remarked: 'And by the way, I see that you have a small relative staying with you – Rosanna Corelli. She told me her name when she brought Monica's belt. She's small for her age, isn't she?'

Bessie's face hardened. She wasn't feeling in a very good temper this evening. Thomas had come home from the works and dropped the bombshell that the departmental managership had been given (over his head) to a young man called Roebottom – a young man who had been sent, at the firm's expense, to the university, and had only a few weeks ago come down with his degree. Of course it was a first-class degree, as Thomas had hastened to add, but still it was shameful (in Bessie's eyes) to pass over Thomas who had been under-manager all these years. And now here was this woman talking of Rosanna being small, as if her Monica was in danger of growing into an elephant. The very idea! Also she remembered Monica's account of yesterday's dancing class, and Mary Martin's favouritism. It was enough to try a saint!

'If you're going to ask me if Rosanna can have dancing

lessons, the answer is No,' she said flatly.

'Is there any particular reason why she should not have them?' persisted Mary, who was a fighter, and who wouldn't own herself beaten. 'Is it the fee, for instance?'

Instantly Bessie saw the trap into which Mary hoped she would fall. If she said yes, the woman would offer to take the child for nothing. Goodness knows *why*, but she could see it coming! Also she had heard of Mary's generosity when it was a case of a promising pupil. But Bessie wasn't having this – she didn't want Rosanna at Monica's dancing class at any price. There must be no competition with her own child.

'No, it isn't the fee,' she said, 'though of course it's true we *should* have found it hard to pay two lots of fees.'

'Well, then—' prompted Mary.

'It's the child's school work,' declared Bessie. (Let Mary get over that one if she could!) 'She's behind as it is – being foreign and that. Her uncle and I have her education to think of – she has her living to earn. She's got her home-work to do, and she has a job to get it done now, without dancing lessons.'

'Rosanna might make dancing her career,' said Mary as a last hope. 'Either on the stage or on the teaching side.'

Bessie smiled – 'a nasty smile' said Mary afterwards to June Robinson, one of her assistants, 'as if she knew full well she had the whip-hand over the poor mite, and intended to use it!'

'I think not,' said Bessie in answer to the dancing mistress. 'The stage is far too precarious. Well, Miss Martin, I think we have discussed the matter of my niece's education long enough. I have a great deal of work to do – we're in the middle of spring cleaning, as you see, so if you will excuse me . . .'

She got up, and Mary could hardly help rising too. Anyway, she felt she had done all she could for the time being. But she did not give up hope. As we have said, she was a fighter. This was only the end of the first round. True, Mrs Waybridge had won it, but there were other rounds to come.

Rosanna came in just ten minutes after Mary Martin had left, to find her aunt's face as black as a thundercloud. Thomas, on his way through the kitchen to the garage, had volunteered the information that young Timothy Roebottom, the new head of the department, was to be given time off to study for his doctorate.

'He's clever, that young chap,' said Thomas (just as if he was *pleased* that a man half his years had been put over his head, thought Bessie in exasperation). 'A nice young man too – no "side" at all.'

'Some people have no pride – that's what it is,' said Bessie. 'Some people are such stick-in-the-muds they couldn't care less if they never got on at all, nor what hardships their families have to endure.'

'What hardships? And what families?' inquired Thomas innocently. 'Is there anything *I* can do to help the poor beggars?'

'*No!*' thundered Mrs Waybridge, goaded beyond endurance. Then she beheld Rosanna, and turned upon her. 'Where have *you* been?' she demanded. 'Look at the time! It's after six o'clock.'

'I've been to tea at Laura's,' said Rosanna. She was so excited, and so full of her own good fortune that she didn't notice the thundercloud upon her aunt's brow. 'Oh, Aunt Bessie, I've got the money for my ballet classes. *You* don't have to pay a penny for them. I've got enough for a whole term.'

There was a moment's silence. Then the storm broke.

'You've *what*? You mean you've been begging again?' (Cyril had told his mother the amusing story of the dancing session outside the theatre and the collecting-box in the church.)

'Oh, no, Aunt. I haven't been begging. It's my own money – truly it is. I sold something of my own to the man in the second-hand shop at the corner of Fenham Road.'

'*What* did you sell?' demanded Bessie, a horrible suspicion coming into her mind.

'I sold some of my clothes – my lace dress, and all the things that went with it.'

'I see,' said Bessie icily. 'And where, if I may ask, had you hidden the clothes?' (She had looked everywhere, it may be said, for the lace dress, because of Monica's school play, but had been unable to find it.)

'I put it in my mattress,' said Rosanna.

There was another silence, while this sank into Mrs Waybridge's almost bemused brain.

'And you sold them – the dress – everything?'

'Yes, Aunt,' said Rosanna. 'And I got enough money for them to pay for my dancing lessons.'

'It will *not*,' thundered Bessie. 'You're to give me the money this instant, and I shall buy something really useful for you – some new school clothes, for instance! Come along – hand it over!'

'I – I can't,' stammered Rosanna, beginning to be a little frightened. Her aunt was looking very strange.

'You can't? How is that?'

'I gave it to Miss Martin.'

'You can't have given it to her,' exclaimed Bessie triumphantly, thinking to catch the child out in a lie. 'Miss Martin has just been here to see me. She left only a few minutes before you came in.'

'I dropped the envelope with the money in through her letterbox,' said Rosanna. 'I wanted her to have it straight away. Oh, please, *please* Aunt Bessie – if you'll only let me have some lessons in ballet, I'll do anything for you – *anything!*'

'I've said No, and I mean No,' said Bessie, remembering what Monica had said – 'Mr Delahaye never took his eyes off her – hadn't a glance for *me*'. No, she wasn't going to risk Rosanna having dancing lessons at Monica's school. One never knew! 'Run away, Rosanna, and let's hear no more of it. I shall write to Miss Martin and ask her for the money back.'

'What's that about asking for money?' said a voice from the door – Thomas's voice.

'Oh, nothing,' said Bessie, shrugging her shoulders, but Rosanna ran to her uncle.

'Oh, Uncle Tom – please let me have some dancing lessons – *please*,' she begged. 'It's all my own money. You see . . .' into his ears she poured the tale of the lace dress, the filmy undergarments, and 'Uncle', who was a pawn-broker and who had given her twenty pounds for them.

'It seems to me to be a reasonable request,' said Thomas, when she had finished. 'If, as she says, the clothes were her own, then the money is her own too, to do as she likes with. I think she might spend it on worse things than dancing lessons.' He put a hand on Rosanna's hair, for just at that moment she had reminded him by some fleeting gesture of her dead mother, his favourite sister Alice. Rosanna felt she had found one friend in the Waybridge household.

'Well, I don't know!' exclaimed Mrs Waybridge in a fury. 'If one can't get support from one's own husband! Oh, well, have it your own way, Thomas, but don't blame *me* for what happens!'

'I won't,' promised Thomas.

Chapter 7

Cynthia Roebottom visits Pit Street

When Cynthia Roebottom, the vicar's wife at Blackheath, that colliery village on the borders of Durham and Northumberland, had discovered (quite by chance) that she had a talent for drawing, things had changed quite a lot for the Roebottom family. First of all Cynthia had concentrated on ballet, drawings inspired by her love for the art, and her interest in the child, Ella Sordy, who had become Ella Rosetti, one of the most famous dancers in the Sadler's Wells Company. But, as the years went on, Cynthia began to draw other things – experimenting in water-colour and oils. Several of her pictures of Blackheath, with its pits, its iron-works and its blast-furnaces had been hung in local art galleries, and she had sold quite half a dozen big canvases. But her delicate water-colours of the ballet always remained prime favourites, and she could sell as many in the Newcastle art shops as she could produce.

Gradually a change had come over the ramshackle vicarage. The threadbare carpets had been replaced with new ones, the plaster no longer flaked off the walls when one walked across the rickety floor. The rooms were now painted in delicate pastel shades, which set off Cynthia's pictures to perfection. Nothing could be done about the uneven floors, of course, since they were the result of colliery workings underneath.

The vicar's wife had changed too – not in character, but in outward appearance. She had given her old brown suit and coat to the parish jumble sale, and was now elegantly (though quietly) dressed in Scottish tweeds of beautiful soft colours – colours that reminded her of that part of Scotland where she had lived as a girl – mist grey, the pink of the heather bell, the blue and mauve of mountain and sea. The vicar had benefited too. His shoes were now the best quality, instead of the cheapest and nastiest, and he had several new surplices of real linen, instead of second-hand cotton ones sent by a charitable body whose duty it was to help poor clergy.

Timothy, the Roebottoms' only son, was on the upgrade too, though as a matter of fact it is true to say that he had turned the corner some years previously, before his mother had begun to make money with her drawings. He had gone up to Cambridge to his father's old college to read history, and had come down without his degree. The truth was he was not really interested in history. Now engineering – that was work for a man! He took his career into his own hands one weekend (quite unknowingly) when he got a job in an engineering and shipbuilding firm on Tyneside. Since then he had never looked back. It wasn't long before he was invited to go back to the 'varsity (King's College, Newcastle, this time) to study engineering at the firm's expense. At first he had refused point-blank, saying that he had lived on his parents long enough, and was now going to help his mother with the household expenses. But it had been pointed out to him that, by getting his degree, he would be able to help his parents a great deal more in the long run, and also that he would be able to work in the 'shops' during the vacations. So he had accepted, and now at the end of two years (since his years at Cambridge had been taken into account) he had come down from King's with first-class honours! He had straight away been made manager of the department in which he had worked before. The under-manager was a man called Waybridge – a decent chap, thought Timothy, but not much of a wizard at engineering! It was odd that he had got as far as he had. Still, he was useful enough in his way – a dependable sort of fellow, and steady as the Bank of England.

Timothy had no girl-friends. He didn't seem to like girls,

106

which was odd, too, when you came to think of it, because it was all too obvious that girls liked *him*! With his tall, graceful figure and his head of fair curls, cut very short now (but no scissors quite got rid of them), not to mention his charm of manner, Timothy Roebottom made every woman he spoke to feel like a princess! But it never got any further. Although of course Timothy met lots of girls at college, he never made 'dates' with any of them. He seemed as if he was far too busy with his career. Or perhaps he still held in his heart the memory of a little girl called Ella Sordy, who had once lived in his colliery village, and whom his mother had befriended, but who had gone away to London and become Ella Rosetti, the famous *ballerina* – far, far too famous for an obscure engineer to dream of marrying. Even if he *had* sometimes thought of it, he drove the idea out of his mind resolutely. You couldn't ask a girl who had the world at her feet to give it all up and settle down to live in a grey, industrial north-country city like Newcastle, could you? Timothy couldn't, anyway – he was far too modest. So he put girls out of his mind, and concentrated on his machines.

But Ella Sordy would not be dismissed. She continued to haunt, if not Timothy, the Roebottom family. One morning Cynthia received a letter from a London publisher who was bringing out a series of books about the lives of famous dancers – Ella Rosetti was one of them. They had got an eminent ballet critic (Oscar Devereux, in fact) to write the text, and they had obtained many excellent photographs of this beautiful dancer in her rôles at Covent Garden. But of her early life they knew little, and they had no photographs of her at all under the age of fifteen. Could Cynthia contact, or write to, Mr Devereux telling him what she knew of the early life of Ella Rosetti? The editor went on to say he understood that Cynthia had made many drawings of Miss Rosetti as a child. He would count it the greatest favour if Mrs Roebottom would augment the text with drawings out of her sketch book, including some of the child's home, if possible. Something intimate would be appreciated.

Nothing pleased Cynthia better. She got out her old sketch book, and, turning over the pages, came upon a set of exquisitely delicate pencil drawings of Ella (aged ten) practising in the church hall – Ella as Cinderella in the school play, Ella dancing at Mary Martin's summer show. She added one she had done as a rough sketch of Ella (some years later) dancing at the parish concert. After this, she put on her hat and set off for Pit Street, which was where the Sordy family lived, and where Ella had spent the first ten years of her life as their adopted child. They had their name down for a new council house, but were still waiting for it.

It was evening, and one of the Sordy daughters (she thought it was Lily) came to the door. Lily worked in the Co-op, appropriately behind the 'fats' counter. She was all dressed up, ready for the local 'hop' in the Co-op dance-hall down the road, and in her tight, black satin sheath dress, she looked, thought Cynthia, like a fat seal which had just come up to breathe. She was pretty in a coarse way, with bouncing flaxen curls, which owed their pallor (though Cynthia did not know it) to the peroxide bottle, and round white neck and arms. Between her bright scarlet lips dangled a cigarette.

'Oh, hullo, Mrs Roebottom,' she said brightly. 'You begging again! Always after summat is the Church. If it ain't for jumbles, it's for the kids' party, or clothes for the heathen. Allus thought the heathen didna wear clothes!' She laughed at her own joke, then stopped for Mrs Roebottom to explain her visit.

'No, I'm not begging this time,' said Cynthia. 'At least not in the usual way. I've been asked to supply some details of Ella Rosetti's life, and also some drawings. I thought that perhaps you—'

'Half a tick,' said Lily. 'I'll ask me Mam—' But before

108

she could turn to go indoors, 'Me Mam', a large, hard-faced woman with her hair in curlers, appeared.

'What's that about our Ella? . . . Oh, it's *you*!' (this to Mrs Roebottom, whom she had never forgiven; for was it not due to that nosy parker, the vicar's wife, that the Sordys had lost Ella and with her the weekly amount they had been paid by the Cottage Homes for looking after her? 'Me Mam' had spent most of that money on 'the pi'tchers', and fish and chips, and had been forced to take a lodger when Ella left. Yes, she felt she had a real grudge against Cynthia Roebottom!)

'I've just explained to Lily – it *is* Lily, isn't it? Children grow up so fast nowadays, one's never sure! – about the drawings I've been asked to do of Miss Rosetti—'

'Our Ella to us, Mrs Roebottom,' broke in Mam Sordy insolently.

'Very well – your Ella, then,' said Cynthia, smiling mildly. (What did it matter *what* the child was called? She was no relative of these Sordys – that was the important point. It didn't hurt Ella if they chose to refer to her as theirs!) 'The fact of the matter is that the editor wants drawings of your house.'

'Our house! I like his bloomin' cheek!' exclaimed Mam Sordy.

'It's a woman editor,' corrected Cynthia. 'Of course if you object I could always do them from memory' (she had, all this time, been making a mental note of as much of the Sordy's front-room as she could see from where she stood), 'but I might miss some of your furnishings, mightn't I? That lovely television set, for instance – it would be a pity to leave *that* out.'

Mam Sordy bridled. If there was anything she was proud of, it was the telly. (She'd been the first in Pit Street to acquire it.)

'Aye, ye can come in and dee yer bit drawings,' she said, relenting a little, 'but ye canna gan upstairs. The room

109

where our Ella slept has been cut in two, for we had to take a lodger, and noo it's nobbut a cupboard!'

Cynthia went inside, and, taking a book out of her pocket, proceeded to make quick sketches of the Sordys' living-room. It had changed quite a bit since Ella had lived there, not entirely for the better, thought Cynthia privately. The open fireplace had given place to a tiled one, and the gleaming steel fender had vanished ('Ower much work to polish it' volunteered Mam Sordy when Cynthia commented upon its absence). The white cat (several years older, of course) had changed its habits with the times, and now lay on the tiled hearth, instead of inside the fender or on top of the oven. The old wooden settle had been replaced by a hideous modern settee covered in imitation leather. Its springs were gone, and it was heaped with cheap velvet cushions, worn threadbare in patches. There was still a 'hookie' mat upon the floor, however, and Mr Alfred Sordy (Lily and D'reen's grandfather) still glowered down upon the television set, as if wondering what on earth (or in heaven) his descendants were up to! The bamboo table was there also, and upon it, instead of a plant with leathery leaves, was a plaster figure similar to the ones in Denton Drive. The Royal Family still held the place of honour on the long wall facing the window, but was flanked by lurid colour prints (given away free in a weekly magazine) of the latest Hollywood film star of the female variety. These prints were not framed, but pinned up with drawing-pins, so that when you tired of one particular star, you could easily tear her down and pin up another!

When Cynthia had finished her sketches, she walked slowly up Pit Street towards Millbank Road, where she would get the bus up the hill home. As she reached the end of the street, a river of molten dross poured down the side of the nearest pit-heap that towered above Blackheath like a great black mountain.

'They're tipping!' thought Cynthia, and stood for a moment lost in wonder at the sight, just as Ella had stood and wondered many and many a night in the past. The lurid red light lit up the whole countryside for miles around, and against the pale evening sky the pit buildings and the grotesque iron-works were silhouetted like something out of another world – a stark world of pulleys, cranes, engine-houses, wheels, and overhead railways. Several enormous egg-shaped cooling-towers dominated the whole. There was a certain romance about it, thought Cynthia, a certain beauty of rugged strength. She pulled her sketch book out again, and, standing under a street lamp – for the light had died down now – she made a quick drawing, with notes down the side as to colours and light and shade. Later she painted a picture in oils which she called 'The Tipping of the Dross', and it was hung in the Laing Art Gallery in Newcastle as 'the work of one of our foremost north-country artists, Mrs Cynthia Roebottom, wife of the vicar of Blackheath, the colliery village which Mrs Roebottom has featured in this masterly canvas'.

As Cynthia waited for the bus she thought a great deal about Ella Rosetti, and wondered whether her son, Timothy, ever thought about her now. She had known, of course, that Timothy had fallen in love with Ella when he was a curly-headed, loose-limbed undergraduate up at Cambridge – Cynthia had keen intuition where her only son was concerned. But she had no idea whether this boy's love had endured and had grown into something deeper. Timothy was not so easy to read, now that he was a man. She sighed, thinking that some day Timothy would bring home a girl and proudly introduce her as his sweetheart. She would dearly have loved that girl to be Ella.

Chapter 8

Ella at Covent Garden

In London Ella was working hard at her dancing. She could not stop now that she was a *ballerina*. In fact, she must work all the harder. Every morning she attended classes with the rest of the company, allowing herself to be criticised and 'pulled to pieces' by the ballet master (or mistress), just as if she were a mere student, or a member of the *corps de ballet*, for such is the discipline the ballet imposes upon those who dedicate themselves to the art. No dancer who cannot bear to be criticised will ever become great.

In the afternoon she had private lessons with one or other of the great teachers – Madame Viret, who had taught Veronica Weston, Maestro Stcherbakof, who had taught Jane Foster, and others. She went to each of them for different things. Madame Viret knew how to strengthen the back and loosen the shoulders, and Stcherbakof, trained in Russia, passed on his big, flowing arm movements to his pupils. At night (when the Sadler's Wells Company was in London) she either danced at Covent Garden, or watched others dance. Night after night she sat – or stood, if there wasn't a spare seat – in the amphitheatre to see the patterns made by *Swan Lake* or *Giselle*, or stood at the back of the grand tier to get a closer view, or in a box to get a close-up of the great dancers, for although she was a great dancer herself, she was still very young and there was a lot she could learn from those others. She watched the incomparable Fonteyn, the dynamic Elvin, the romantic Weston, all interpreting the same classic rôles in entirely different ways, just as she herself would interpret them in yet another way. It was very fascinating.

Between her dancing on stage and her practising, there were photograph sessions to be fitted in, interviews with the press, with editors of magazines, besides the numerous stage costumes to be tried on and fitted. So it will be seen that the life of a *ballerina* is a busy one, although it must be said, also, that Ella enjoyed every hectic minute! At night she fell into the dreamless sleep of one who is tired, but who enjoys perfect physical health, happy in mind and body. A lot was due to Lady Bailey, in whose house Ella still lived, and who saw to it that proper meals were forthcoming at all times of the day or night for the dancers living under her roof.

She had begun her career as a *ballerina* by dancing the leading rôle in the classical ballet – *Lac des Cygnes* – at a matinée performance, as is the general rule at the Wells. She had been totally unknown, and no one had sung her praises, or publicised her in any way beforehand, so that when the audience acclaimed her, they recognised in her those qualities that go to make up a *ballerina*, and which mark her out from a mere soloist, that indefinable 'something' – call it authority, personality, what you will – that fills the stage, and takes precedence over all the other dancers. It is something that is born in a dancer, and cannot be made, though it can be brought out and fostered.

Ella did not always dance the main rôles at Covent Garden. Sometimes she danced the Lilac Fairy in the *Sleeping Beauty*, or Myrtha, Queen of the Wilis, in *Giselle*. Sometimes she was one of the three soloists in *Les Sylphides*. The rôle that delighted her audiences most (and became her own) was that of the title rôle in the ballet *Cinderella*, and that is hardly to be wondered at, since was she not something of a Cinderella herself, living as she had for the first ten years of her life at the foot of the slag-heaps in a family where there were two sisters, not ugly, perhaps, but not exactly beautiful? Veronica Weston had been her fairy godmother, who had taken her from that pit village, and set her feet upon the stage, and there had been a fairy prince too – a fair-haired boy of eighteen called Timothy Roebottom, who had bought for her her very first ballet dress for her very first ballet, and that, strangely enough, had been *Cinderella* too! No wonder Ella loved this romantic fairy-tale.

One July day, at the end of the ballet season, Ella danced the main rôle in *The Firebird* for the first time. At the end of the performance – which was the last, for the next day was Sunday – she received the usual floral tributes, but conspicuous among them was a beautiful bouquet of velvety white roses. Although she could not see the occupants of the boxes, she knew that in one of them, watching her at this very moment as she stood in front of the curtain, curtsying first to one side, then to the other, was an olive-skinned young man with a star upon his breast – the exiled king of Slavonia. She had read, of course, of his dramatic flight from his kingdom, the destruction of his royal palace, and the breaking of his engagement to his cousin, the Grand Duchess Sopheodorovitch. For a while she had been apprehensive, but as time went on she had come to the conclusion that His Majesty had forgotten her – that she had been just another dancer who had captured his fancy for a while, to be quickly replaced by someone else, an actress or film star, maybe.

The fact was that the young man had waited with unusual patience until he had learned that his cousin, the Grand Duchess, really was married to Ludwig Oppenheim before contacting Ella again. But he had not forgotten her, nor had he lost sight of her for a moment. When the company had gone on tour, King Leopold followed (in his private plane). From a box, or from the stalls, he had watched Ella in every rôle she danced, becoming more and more enchanted with her. At last he had received the information he waited for – the news of his cousin's marriage. He need wait no longer. He could woo and win Ella Rosetti as a free man. That he might *not* win her simply never occurred to him.

As for Ella – her heart was filled with dismay. King Leopold had *not* forgotten her. He was here in this very theatre, and soon she would have to face him. As she smiled and curtsied to the audience thoughts raced through her brain. He would not take no for an answer, now that he was free to marry whomever he wished – she was sure of that! Terror filled her. She must manage to leave the theatre unseen, and thus put off the evil day!

In her dressing-room his card, surmounted by the familiar crest – the golden wolves on the sable field – awaited her. It was, as usual, more of a command than a request – he would be pleased to dine with Miss Rosetti at the Carlton. Ella scribbled a brief: 'So sorry, but am otherwise engaged this evening', signed it, and gave it to her dresser, who in turn passed it on to a call-boy to deliver. It was quite true – she *was* otherwise engaged, she told herself guiltily. She had to go home, pack her things, and go early to bed, for tomorrow she was catching the morning train to Northumberland. There was to be a special ballet performance at Hordon Castle sponsored by several of her dearest friends – Mariella Campbell (Foster, before her marriage) and Jane Charlton, who had given up her ballet career and left the Wells to become the wife of Guy Charlton, the veterinary surgeon. The Charltons and the Campbells both lived at Hordon Castle, which belonged to Guy's father and had been in the Charlton family for many generations. Old Mr Charlton had a wing of the ancient fortress where he lived himself.

Ella had promised long ago that she would dance at the Evening of Ballet, and now it was going to prove very convenient. The young king would never guess where she had gone!

She left the theatre by ways known only to those who work there, and came out into a dark street somewhere at the back of the great Opera House. Peeping round the corner she could see a long black car drawn up to the stage-door. Although she was not near enough to distinguish it, she knew by instinct that it bore upon the panels of its highly polished door the royal arms of Slavonia. Then he was still waiting for her! There seemed something ominous about it. Oh, well, the ballet season was finished, and tomorrow she was off to the wilds of Northumberland, and there she would stay until her holiday was over. Leopold would never find her there. Alas for Ella! – she was reck-oning without the long arm of coincidence.

Chapter 9

Life is Difficult for Rosanna

At first, as we have said, Bessie Waybridge was not actually hostile towards Rosanna. Most of the time she ignored her, or treated her as an unpaid domestic, giving her the vegetables to peel, the silver to polish, the dishes to wash. In fact, though she wouldn't have admitted it, Bessie found the child quite useful. She wouldn't have admitted either than Rosanna was a good deal more obliging about doing chores than her own daughter. It wasn't until Rosanna began to attend the Mary Martin ballet school that Bessie found herself actively disliking her niece. The truth was that Rosanna had become a rival to Monica and Bessie brooked no rivals to her beloved children. Mary Martin was partly to blame – quite unintentionally, of course – by moving Rosanna into a higher class than Monica. And then the one class a week became two (at no extra charge), and after this an agreement was made between Mary and Rosanna that the latter would go along on Saturday mornings and help with the little ones, in return for which she would be allowed to attend any classes she wished on the other days of the week. So nearly every night found Rosanna practising in Mary's small studio, or dancing with the students in the big one. She progressed enormously, and was more beautiful to watch than ever. She became almost happy.

Bessie, on the other hand, grew more and more disgruntled. Thomas wasn't making any more headway at his work. He seemed to be stuck, and moreover he seemed quite happy to be stuck. That young Roebottom was taking all the credit for work that Thomas did (Bessie's opinion, but far from the truth). And now the crowning insult had come. A ship was nearing completion, and the launching ceremony was being performed by a certain Duchess of Darlington, who was the sister of a foreign royalty. This lady and her royal brother were to inspect the workshops also, and the person chosen to conduct the illustrious visitors round the vast shipyard was – not Thomas, but that same young upstart (Bessie's words), Timothy Roebottom! No wonder Bessie was in a bad temper. No wonder she vented her spleen on the nearest thing to hand – and the most defenceless – Rosanna!

'These dancing classes!' she exploded. 'There are far too many of them, Rosanna. You do nothing but dance, dance, dance, morning, noon, and night! It's got to be a mania with you. In short, it's got to stop.'

Rosanna was too horrified to say anything, so Bessie went on.

'I get no work at all out of you nowadays, and after all your uncle and I have done for you, it's sheer ingratitude.'

'What did you want doing?' asked Rosanna.

'Don't be impertinent!' thundered Mrs Waybridge.

117

'Oh, but I'm *not*,' said Rosanna truthfully. 'I'll do anything for you, Aunt – anything, so long as you'll let me go on dancing. I've peeled the vegetables every day before my class, but if you want any more done, or you'll just leave the washing-up, I'll do it when I come back—'

'What! And leave all those dirty dishes standing in the sink? No, Rosanna, it won't do. All these classes must stop.' Bessie Waybridge knew enough about ballet (through hearing Monica talk) to realise that if you intend to make it your career, you must have at least one class a day. *She'd* see that Rosanna didn't get her daily class! Nobody was going to push her Monica to the wall! Let anyone try, that's all! She daren't stop Rosanna's dancing lessons altogether because of Thomas, but Thomas, not knowing the first thing about ballet, would imagine that two classes per week were more than enough. He wouldn't risk upsetting his wife by upholding Rosanna in her demand for more.

Poor Mary Martin was dismayed.

'Only *two* classes a week! Oh, Rosanna, is that all you can manage? It's not enough, and you were getting on so well – so very well.'

'It's my aunt,' said Rosanna (as if Mary didn't know it). 'You see, she – I don't think she really likes me taking up ballet as my career.'

Mary said nothing to this. It didn't do to discuss parents and relatives with the children. But her thoughts (so she told June Robinson afterwards) would have lit a bonfire!

Mary had her plans for Rosanna, and now here was this wretched woman, her aunt, upsetting them all! At the end of July, just before dancing school broke up, there was to be an Evening of Ballet at Hordon Castle, the home of one of her former pupils, Jane Foster. Another of her former pupils, Veronica Weston, that most lyrical of *ballerinas*, would be there too and Mary had been asked to supply a ballet of children. Now Mary knew that Rosanna had merely to obtain an audition for the Sadler's Wells School

118

and she would be accepted as a pupil, but she knew also that Bessie Waybridge would not allow her niece to go to London to that audition, even if Mary paid the child's train fare out of her own pocket, which she would not have hesitated to do. Bessie would, in fact (Mary knew it now) go to any lengths to stop Rosanna obtaining any such audition. So the Evening of Ballet at Hordon Castle was to be Rosanna's audition. If she was seen, and approved of, by Miss Weston herself, that would be enough. She would be granted a scholarship, which Bessie could hardly refuse, and Mary Martin would have given one more dancer (who without her help would never have been heard of) to the world.

Mary had already worked out a delightful little ballet – an adaptation of Hans Andersen's *The Emperor's Nightingale*, and Rosanna should dance in it and it should be the turning-point in her career. She didn't reveal her plan to the child – there was always the chance of slip betwixt cup and lip, and she didn't want Rosanna to be disappointed. None of the students, in fact, knew that the affair was anything more than 'just another show'. Thus Mary would see which of them worked without the incentive of knowing that Sadler's Wells dancers would be present at the soirée. There were those pupils (Mary really knew them already) who only really worked their hardest when there was someone whom they considered worthwhile to show off to. Monica Waybridge, for instance. If there was an R.A.D. free class, Monica would be in the front row; if it was a case of a special show of any sort, Monica would turn up at the last three rehearsals, having 'cut' most of the ones before. At the dress rehearsal there she would be in a brand new ballet frock, but only half-knowing the dances. Monica Waybridge was not, in fact, proving very satisfactory, which was a pity, thought Mary, because her dancing was quite good. Not in the same class as Rosanna's, of course, but she had her moments of inspiration. Mary (partly as a

119

sop to Bessie and partly because she thought the rôle a suitable one) intended to give the part of the Mechanical Nightingale to Monica.

And so Mary schemed, forgetting that 'the best-laid plans often go awry' especially when there are jealous women concerned.

'Oh, well,' she said to Rosanna, 'if you can't manage more, I suppose you can't, but if your aunt *does* relent and let you have an odd evening, just come along, and we'll make the most of it!'

'Oh, I will, Miss Martin, you can be sure I will,' Rosanna promised. 'I'll come whenever I can.' So whenever Mrs Waybridge went out to her Ladies' Club, or on a prolonged shopping expedition, and Monica wasn't about, Rosanna dashed off to the ballet school in Rothbury Crescent. Sometimes Monica came out as she went in, but she was careful to keep out of sight. I'm afraid a lot of deceit went into all this, Rosanna pretending she had been with her friend Laura Montessori, when really she had been dancing, but it was harmless deceit, and you must admit that there was every excuse for Rosanna. Moreover, she remembered Anya Boccaccio's words on her last evening at Amalfi: 'Your dancing must come first, Rosanna, in all that you do.'

Well, she was seeing that it did!

When you dislike someone for a specific reason, everything that person does and everything connected with them annoys you. Bessie began to dislike the very look of Rosanna. It annoyed her when the child's cheeks filled out, and her eyes became clear and sparkling as she grew happier. Partly it was due to the weather – Italians are notoriously affected by the weather – which grew warmer, but principally, of course, it was due to her dancing and her friendship with Mary Martin.

The Montessoris came in for Bessie's displeasure too. She'd found out by now that Rosanna had made a friend of the little Montessori girl, and at first she'd been only too glad to get rid of Rosanna. But after the episode of the lace dress she'd changed her mind. The Montessoris, she said to herself, had acted disgracefully in that affair, encouraging Rosanna to do something which they knew full well would not have the approval of her aunt. And anyway, the Montessoris were Italians, and Bessie didn't like foreigners of any sort. She tackled Rosanna about her friends.

'This Italian family with the ice-cream shop,' she began. 'They're no fit friends for you, Rosanna. When your uncle and I moved from the council estate, we gave up associating with *that* sort of person. Why, Mr Montessori goes round with a cart selling his own ice-cream. I've seen him!'

'Oh, yes, I know he does, Aunt,' cried Rosanna, springing gallantly to the defence of her friends. She could indeed see nothing shameful in a man wanting to sell his own wares. 'Antonio loves going round with his van. You see he's ever so proud of his ice-cream – it's the best for miles around, and it's made from a recipe that was handed down to him by his father, and his grandfather before that. Besides, he meets all his friends—'

'Well, I hope he doesn't count *me* as one of them,' said Bessie with high disdain. 'Here have I been slaving for years to raise Thomas's family from the dust, and now you must come and drag it in the mud again by making friends with these Italians.'

'Oh, but they're ever such nice people,' pleaded Rosanna. 'Really, Aunt, you can't think what nice, good people they are.'

'You must allow *me* to be the judge of that,' said Bessie. 'I'm a great deal older and wiser than you are, my dear, and if I say that the Montessori family are no fit friends for you, you must realise that I have my reasons for saying so.'

'If you're meaning about the pawnbroker—' began Rosanna, then stopped because her aunt's face had grown quite red with anger.

'Yes, I *was* meaning about the pawnbroker,' cried Mrs Waybridge. 'I wasn't going to mention it, but now you've done so, I must say that of all the disgraceful things I've ever heard of – to introduce a trusting child to a common pawnbroker! Well, Rosanna, that episode is just one of many which prove that your friendship with these people must stop. Of course I can't forbid you to speak to the little girl – whatever her name is' – Bessie knew Laura's name quite well, but chose to pretend she didn't – 'since she attends the same school, but I can, and do, forbid you to go to their dirty house.'

'It *isn't* dirty!' cried Rosanna, unable to bear hearing her dearest friends so insulted. 'It's the cleanest house you ever saw, and the most beautiful!' Her eyes filled with tears at the thought of the Montessoris' warm living-room with its bead curtains.

'I suppose,' said Bessie sarcastically, 'that it's a great deal more beautiful than this one?'

Rosanna certainly thought it was, but she had more sense than to say so. She was silent.

'Well, whether it is or not, the fact remains, the Montessoris are just common people,' declared Bessie, 'and foreigners at that, and I forbid you to go there again. Understand, Rosanna?'

Poor Rosanna nodded silently. She couldn't speak, or she would have burst into tears. Next to Giorgio, and Anya, and Mary Martin, the Montessoris were the people she loved best in the whole world, and now she would have to tell them she couldn't go to their house any more. It would hurt them deeply, she knew. Yet what could she do? While she lived at Hayfield Lodge she must obey her aunt.

Chapter 10

The New Ballet

Mary's ballet, *The Emperor's Nightingale*, was adapted freely from Hans Andersen's famous fairy-tale. That is to say she had followed the story closely, but had given the ballet a classical setting, dressing her dancers in classical costumes and not in Chinese clothes. A Chinese setting, let alone Chinese music, would have been too difficult for them.

The story goes that in China there lived a powerful Emperor. Tales reached his court that in the distant woods of his own kingdom there dwelt a fabulous bird – a nightingale – who sang so sweetly that it was a delight to hear her. So the Emperor sent one of his courtiers to find the bird and bring her to the palace. To the surprise of everyone the nightingale proved to be a modest, grey little bird – not at all the magnificent creature they had expected. However, they were all delighted with her song, and the Emperor had a golden cage made for her, so that she could live at the palace always. Indeed she could not escape, for a silken cord was fastened round her leg.

One day a parcel arrived for the Emperor from the Emperor of Japan – an artificial nightingale. It was covered with diamonds, rubies, and sapphires, and when it was wound up it imitated the real nightingale's song to perfection. When it trilled, its tail, sparkling with gold and silver, wagged up and down. Oh, it was a splendid sight! The Emperor and his courtiers were so delighted with the costly gift that they forgot all about the real bird, and she slipped the knot of the silken cord, and flew out of the window of the palace back to her shady woods, and no one missed her. Not at first, anyway, and when they did, they were consoled by the magnificence of the artificial nightingale who would sing for hours without ever getting tired.

For some time the artificial nightingale enchanted the court, and then one day something happened – the clockwork began to wear out! The court watchmaker pronounced that the greatest care must be taken of the jewelled songster, and in order not to put too great a strain upon the works, she was only allowed to sing once a year.

Five years later, a dreadful tragedy occurred. The Emperor fell ill, and was not expected to recover. Indeed, thinking him already dead, the courtiers had run away to pay their respects to his successor. Lying in his great bed, the Emperor saw Death approach, crowned with his own crown, and carrying his own sceptre, whilst round his bed gathered a ghostly throng – all his good and bad deeds. There were a great deal more of the former, I am glad to say, than of the latter.

The Emperor cried aloud for music, so that he could not hear Death's voice in his ear, but the artificial nightingale was silent. There was nobody to wind her up! And then suddenly a wonderful sound filled the room. It was the real nightingale, who had heard of her Emperor's illness and had come to cheer him. As she sang, the ghosts returned to the shadows and faded away, and gradually strength began to flow back into the sick Emperor's limbs. Even Death himself gave up the Emperor's crown for one of the nightingale's beautiful songs. The nightingale sang of the quiet burial-ground where the sweet white roses grow, and the grass is bedewed with the tears of the mourners, so that Death was seized with such a longing for his own garden that, like a cold white mist, he floated out of the window and vanished. At this very moment the fickle courtiers reappeared to pay a last tribute to their dead Emperor. Imagine their surprise when their Emperor sat up and said, 'Good morning!'

Like so many choreographers, Mary had a certain dancer in mind when she composed her ballet, and this dancer was

Rosanna Corelli. Rosanna was to be the Real Nightingale, and all her solos were designed especially to show off her best points – the pure line of her *arabesque*, her beautiful, unaffected hands, her neat footwork, her 'large' *portes de bras*, which had no ugly angles to mar them, and the lyrical appeal of her dancing altogether. The Artificial Nightingale was a showy rôle, and it was not surprising that Monica Waybridge, who hadn't bothered to read the fairy-tale, was deceived into thinking that Mary had given the principal rôle to *her*!

'Mum! Mum!' she cried, bursting into the kitchen. 'I've got the chief rôle in the ballet! The best rôle of all. Oh, I have the most wonderful dances to do, and I'm to wear a jade green *tutu*, glittering with rubies, sapphires, and diamonds – sequins, of course. I told Miss Martin I could have a new one – a new *tutu*, I mean. I can, can't I? Everyone's having new ones. Oh, and Miss Martin asked about Rosanna – she's the other Nightingale, and it's an awfully dull part – and I told her Rosanna could have my old white *tutu*.'

'Yes, of course, you can have a new *tutu*, my pet,' said Bessie, and if she had been a cat you would have heard her purring with satisfaction. 'And, yes, I dare say Rosanna can wear your old one – it's certainly past its best!'

So the dressmaker who made all the *tutus* and costumes for the Mary Martin School was commissioned to make a new *tutu* for Monica. After it was finished everyone at Hayfield Lodge was deputed to sew on sequins of red, blue, and silver, until you couldn't look at the dress without blinking. When Monica took it along to Mary and proudly showed it to her, Mary smiled and nodded. Yes, it was just right – exactly the effect she wanted for that particular rôle – hard, glittering, artificial.

'And Mum says Rosanna can wear my old white *tutu*,' stated Monica, producing out of her case a mass of crushed off-white net and tarlatan. 'It can be ironed last thing before

125

the performance, but I brought it along now because it takes up such a lot of room in my wardrobe.'

'Oh – er, thank you, Monica,' said Mary, glancing at the frock with mentally raised eyebrows. 'Yes, that will do nicely.' She added to herself: 'For rehearsals, that is, but as for the actual performance – well, we'll see!'

Later on Mary talked to Rosanna about the ballet.

'I've given you the chief rôle,' she said. 'It's that of the Nightingale. I was really thinking of you when I composed the ballet, and I want you to put your very best work into it (although I know you always do that, my dear) because much more depends upon your dancing in this ballet performance than you know. I can't say more just now.'

'Yes, Miss Martin,' said Rosanna. 'I'll do my very best.'

'You still can't manage more than two classes a week?' questioned Mary.

'No, I'm afraid not,' answered Rosanna.

'Well, I'll get Jill Wainwright to understudy you,' said Mary. 'She can dance the rôle at all the rehearsals which you can't atttend. I'll let her dance the Nightingale at our end-of-term show at the Theatre Metropole, then she won't feel aggrieved. But you, Rosanna, and you only, must dance this rôle at Hordon Castle. I'll give you a private coaching lesson either before or after each rehearsal, and that ought to meet the case. Oh, and another thing,' added Mary, 'this ballet-dress of your cousin's that she's offered to lend you – it's very old and dirty, isn't it?'

'I'll wash it,' said Rosanna eagerly. 'I'll iron it most carefully—'

'No, I think not,' said Mary firmly. 'The money, Rosanna, that you sent me for your classes – I kept it because I thought it might come in useful, not because I wanted to be paid for teaching you. Well, now you see it *has* come in useful. We'll buy some nylon net and make you a new *tutu*. Don't tell anyone about it, though,' cautioned the artful Mary. 'It will be a great surprise.'

It was! The night before the show Monica arrived home from the dress-rehearsal in a towering rage.

'Mum! D'you know what! Miss Martin has given Rosanna a new *tutu*, and it's the most fabulous one you ever saw! Real nylon net, pale grey, and it looks – oh, I can't describe it, but none of us look *anything* beside Rosanna. And I found out quite by chance that Rosanna's been having private coaching lessons before the rehearsals, and Miss Martin has let her do all sorts of wonderful things, even triple *pirouettes*, in her *solos* that Jill Wainwright never does. It isn't fair! Rosanna looks like the *prima ballerina*, and everyone else like the mere *corps de ballet*. Somehow Mary's made *her* into the chief dancer in the ballet, and it ought to be *me*! I've learnt far longer than she has, in fact I began years and years before Rosanna. Oh, Mum, you never ought to have let her go to Mary Martin's. I know it was partly Dad's fault, but surely you could have done *something*. Rosanna'll get to the Wells – *you'll* see! I believe Mary Martin intends it. I believe she's put on this show so as to get her there. All sorts of V.I.P.s are going to be there – Veronica Weston, for one, and Ella Rosetti, too. Miss Weston only has to *see* Rosanna in that wonderful new *tutu*, and doing all those *pirouettes* and things, and she'll accept her for the Wells School straight away. Give her a scholarship, I shouldn't wonder! She won't even see *me*, and *you'll* be to blame!'

Monica, as can be seen, had learned a lot during this last rehearsal. Mary had thought it safe to let out her secret, and now the whole school knew the glorious news – that Veronica Weston was to see the ballet, and also Ella Rosetti, another famous Wells *ballerina*.

All the time Monica had been speaking, Bessie's face had been growing darker and darker. So Mary Martin had double-crossed her after all, and was aiming to push Rosanna Corelli – that little Italian upstart – in front of her Monica! Well, it remained to be seen who was the stronger

– Bessie Waybridge or Mary Martin.

'Where is Rosanna now? She ought to be home,' she demanded. 'I suppose she's having another dancing lesson on the quiet!'

'No,' said a voice from the door – Cyril's voice. 'She isn't having a dancing lesson, my dear Mama. Shall I tell you where your precious Rosanna is? She's in the Montessoris' house. Yes, I saw her go off in that direction this afternoon after school, so I followed her just to make sure, and there she'll be right now.'

'Now that's very interesting, Cyril, very interesting indeed,' said his mother.

'I don't see that it's interesting a bit,' pouted Monica, full of her own grievances. 'What does Rosanna, and where she goes, matter? What does anything matter except the fact that Rosanna's going to look miles better than me tomorrow night, and it's all *your* fault!'

'Hush, my pet!' said Bessie. 'Something may yet be done. Cyril, you have given me an idea.'

And now we must go back a few hours, to that morning when Rosanna had arrived at the school gates, and had been met by a white-faced Laura.

'Oh, Rosanna, would you tell Miss Dixon, I'm not coming to school this morning. She won't kick up a fuss because it's the last day of term, and could you tidy out my part of our desk. I wouldn't ask you only . . .' She began to cry.

'What's the matter?' asked Rosanna. 'Is something wrong at home?'

'It's Mum,' gulped Laura. 'She's been taken bad. She's got to go to hospital early tomorrow for an operation. It's terribly serious. Mrs Golightly says she won't get over it, and it's just a matter of time.' (Mrs Golightly lived next door to the Montessoris.) 'She says not one in a hundred do.'

'Don't take any notice of Mrs Golightly,' said Rosanna, though she herself would have been the first to do so, but she felt she must console her friend somehow. 'I don't expect she really knows much about it.'

'Oh, Rosanna, I hate to ask you to do this,' went on Laura, 'but *could* you come and see Mum before she goes? She's been asking for you, and getting herself in such a state because you haven't been to see her.'

'Doesn't she know why? Didn't you tell her?' said Rosanna.

'Yes, of course I did, but now she's so ill she seems to have forgotten. She's all in a daze, and she keeps on moaning and saying that even *you* have forgotten her. Oh, Rosanna, please, *please* come and see her. It will make her so happy, and surely it can't be wrong for you to come just this once. It will have to be today though, because the ambulance is coming early in the morning.'

'I'll come,' promised Rosanna. As Laura said, surely it couldn't be wrong under the circumstances? Even her aunt wouldn't be angry if she knew how dreadfully ill poor Mrs Montessori was. Anyhow, she would never know. It was certainly hard luck on Rosanna that Cyril Waybridge happened to see her and follow her on that particular afternoon.

Chapter 11

The Blow Falls

All that night Bessie lashed herself into a fury. By morning she had made herself believe that Rosanna was a bundle of deceit and wickedness, that she had, like the cuckoo, turned Monica and Cyril out of their own nest, and usurped their places. She must be punished – that was certain! She must learn that her aunt's commands were law, and not to be broken with impunity. She waited until Thomas had gone off to his work – somewhat earlier than usual, because this was an important day, the day on which royalty was to launch the ship and inspect the yards. Although Thomas wasn't conducting the important visitors round the 'shops', he still, as deputy manager, had to be there early to see that everything was ship-shape. He was absent-minded during breakfast, his mind already down in the great shipyard, or he would have noticed that Bessie's mouth was nipped in even tighter than usual, and that there was a strange air of waiting-for-something-to-happen hanging over the house. Rosanna also was too absent-minded to notice anything wrong; her thoughts were with poor Elena Montessori, tossing and moaning on her bed. Just at this moment the ambulance would be coming for her. Rosanna was so used to fate dealing her cruel blows that she was resigned to receiving yet another one – the loss of her dear friend, Elena Montessori. She knew quite well that she would not recover.

Meanwhile Thomas had brushed his hat rather more carefully than usual, shrugged on his coat, and shut the front door carefully behind him. He nodded a 'good morning' to George Higginbottom across the fence, wishing that Bessie would let him be friends with the people next door. They seemed real decent folk, but of course it wasn't worth having a scene with his wife. As the garden gate clanged after him, Bessie turned to Rosanna and said in a furious voice:

'And where were you yesterday, Rosanna, if I might ask?'

'Yesterday?' echoed the child, her thoughts coming back to Hayfield Lodge with a jolt.

'Yes,' said Bessie. 'Yesterday. I'll answer that question myself and save you lying to me. You were at the Montessoris. You needn't bother to deny it, because you were seen going there.'

'Oh, yes, I *was* there,' answered Rosanna. 'You see, Aunt, Mrs Montessori is very ill – she's going to the hospital this morning early in the ambulance, and she wanted to see me before she went. Oh, Aunt – poor, poor Mrs Montessori is dying!'

'Dying my foot!' exclaimed Bessie. 'What a lot of rubbish! I know these people. They make a fuss over the slightest thing. You had no right to go there, Rosanna, against my express orders.'

'I would have asked you, Aunt,' said Rosanna, 'but you see there wasn't time.' She might have added: 'Besides, I was afraid you'd refuse.'

'You realise, don't you, that you must be punished for your disobedience?' went on Bessie.

'Yes, Aunt. I'll wash as many dishes as you want – at least I will after the show today. . . .'

'After today! After today!' broke in Bessie. 'Yes, there you have it, Rosanna! You put your own wishes first always. You wanted your dancing lessons, so you got them by most underhand means; you wanted to go to the Montessoris, so you went against my wishes; you wanted a new frock for the ballet, throwing aside the frock Monica so kindly lent you. You haven't a spark of gratitude in you.'

'But Miss Martin said – I mean she offered—' began

Rosanna. But Bessie cut her short.

'Mary Martin is another deceitful person,' she thundered, working herself up into a bigger rage every minute. 'I've a good mind to take Monica away from her.' (Nothing in fact was further from her thoughts; Mary was far too good a teacher, and far too cheap!) 'Oh, well,' she ended, 'there's only one punishment that will teach you where your duty lies, Rosanna. You will not take part in the Evening of Ballet tonight at Hordon Castle. You will clean the silver instead! Then perhaps next time you will remember that I mean what I say.'

'Well,' said Cyril Waybridge's voice from the door, 'I'll be off!' His school didn't break up until next day. ''Bye, everybody!' He had just waited until Mum had delivered the death-blow. He wanted to see Rosanna's stricken face when it fell. Cyril Waybridge was the sort of boy who pulls the wings off flies to see them wriggle!

Chapter 12

The Boy Next Door

The ballet students were to assemble at Mary Martin's at one o'clock, when they would be taken to Hordon (a distance of some forty miles) by bus. There was to be a run-through of the whole performance at three-thirty, which would be attended by all the village children, and anyone else who couldn't come in the evening. You might really call it a matinée performance. After this was over, there was to be tea and a rest for the dancers before the evening performance, which was at seven-thirty. This programme left them plenty of time to see the wonderful rock-gardens that had been made down in Hordon Dene, and everyone, especially the grown-ups, was looking forward to seeing them.

From her box-room window, Rosanna watched Monica and her mother set out for the ballet-school at about a quarter to one. Cyril hadn't come in to lunch, so the house was silent and empty. She crept downstairs, her mind numb with despair. The kitchen looked as if a cyclone had struck it – dirty dishes littered the table, clothes lay on all the chairs. Monica and her mother had evidently had a hard job to decide which clothes to wear for the important occasion. They had dashed out leaving the scullery window open, and the Higginbottoms' cat (they had two cats, and a dog as well) had squeezed in and upset the milk-jug. The milk had streamed across the table-cloth, and was dripping in a miniature waterfall on to the floor, where Tibby, the cat, was lapping it up contentedly. She looked up as Rosanna came in, then, seeing that it wasn't Mrs Waybridge (who always chased her away), went on lapping shamelessly.

'Oh, Tibby!' said Rosanna, putting her arms round the marauder, and laying her hot cheek against the cat's spotless white waistcoat, 'I'm so very, very miserable!'

After a few moments she got up and began to wash the dishes and put the room straight. While she did this, her mind came out of its anaesthetic, and stabs of pain shot through her heart. Why, why should she stay in this horrible house? She would be better at home, in Amalfi, where, even if she had no money and had to walk barefoot, at least she had kind, friendly people to talk to. Even as regards her dancing, she was in a worse plight here in England, for she knew (yes, she knew quite certainly now) that Mrs Waybridge would never let her make ballet her career, since by doing so she would be rivalling Monica.

Suddenly Rosanna made up her mind: she would go back to Italy, and work for Anya Boccaccio as a maid, in return for dancing lessons. She was sure Anya would agree. The question was – how to get there? She had no money and moreover no passport, for her aunt had taken charge of that when she had arrived. The only thing left to her was to become a stowaway. Her mind went back to the great liner, *Colonsay*, in which she had travelled to England. There were, she was sure, lots and lots of places where she could hide. Yes, when she had finished the washing-up, she would go down to the docks and find a ship, and never, never return to this hateful house. Hot tears began to fall on the clean plates, so that she had to dry them again.

Having finished the dishes, Rosanna went upstairs once more. There was one good thing about being a stowaway – you didn't need any luggage! There were one or two things, however, that she must take with her. From under her mattress she pulled out the letters Anya had sent her, and Giorgio's photograph. She didn't want the Waybridges to find them. She hid the photograph inside her dress, and took the letters down to the kitchen, where she put them in the stove.

She was now ready to go. The question was how to get out of Hayfield Lodge. Bessie had taken the back-door key with her, and locked the front door behind her, hiding the key underneath the scraper where Thomas would know where to find it when he came home in the evening. It was obvious that Bessie was taking no chances of Rosanna following on to Hordon by herself! Well, there was only one thing to do – she must climb out of the window. The trouble was they were all casement windows, and the part that opened very long and narrow – impossible even for anyone as small as Rosanna to squeeze through. But the scullery window was of a different pattern, and it looked possible. She climbed on to the draining-board, and opened the window to its full extent, while Tibby watched her curiously with interested amber eyes. She'd never seen a human being climb through a window before. Windows were for cats on the prowl, not humans!

But even the scullery window proved to be too small. Rosanna stuck, half in and half out, her shoulders wedged in the narrow opening. She could go neither forwards nor backwards. It was at this awkward moment that a boy's voice (with what Bessie Waybridge called a 'la-de-da' accent) said politely: 'Excuse me, but wouldn't it be easier to go round by the door?'

Rosanna raised her head with some difficulty, and looked round in the direction of the voice. The boy from the house next door (not the Higginbottoms', but the Johnsons') was standing on the far side of the fence that divided their back gardens. From her elevated position Rosanna could see that he was carrying a canvas bag, so she knew (from Cyril) that he was going to play cricket.

'My aunt has taken the back-door key with her,' she said, 'and she's locked the front door and put the key under the scraper.'

'Oh, I see. She's locked you in?' said the boy. 'I take it you're breaking out? Well, I wish you luck. How you've stood the old gorgon as long as you have beats me! Supposing I find the key, let myself in, and pull you back. You seem to be in a bit of a jam!'

'Thank you, that would be nice of you,' said Rosanna. 'It's under the scraper at the corner of the porch – the key, I mean.'

'O.K.,' said the boy. 'I know it! I've watched the old gorgon putting it there many a time! My name's Iain Thompson, as I expect you know.'

Rosanna nodded as well as she could. She wondered what he thought about things as he vaulted over the fence and went whistling round to the front door. As a matter of fact Iain was intrigued. He had no love for the Waybridges as a family. He thought Bessie a harridan, Cyril a bounder, and Monica a brat. The old man – well, he wasn't a bad old stick! Weak of character, though, to let himself be pushed around by his objectionable family. The little Italian girl who had come to live with the Waybridges seemed harmless enough – he hadn't quite made up his mind about her, though he liked to watch her move. Graceful kid! She looked miserable as a wet weekend at the moment, stuck half in and half out of the window. He wondered what had happened. He'd like to bet there'd been the dickens of a row. Perhaps she was running away back to Italy. He decided to ask her.

'Look,' he said, when he had managed to pull Rosanna back into the scullery, 'if you don't mind my asking – where are you running away to? I gather you *are* running away?'

'I'm going back to Italy,' said Rosanna. After all, why shouldn't he know? She was quite sure he wasn't the sort of boy to tell tales, and it was a relief to talk to someone.

'By air possibly?' said Iain. He was being lightly sarcastic, but Rosanna took him quite seriously.

'Oh, no, that would be much too expensive,' she answered. 'Besides, I haven't got a passport.'

'No passport?' echoed the boy, with a lift of his eyebrows. 'Distinct snag, I'd say, whichever way you propose to travel. Unless perhaps you're thinking of being a stowaway?' Again he was being sarcastic. One read in the papers and in adventure stories about stowaways, but one never met them. To his astonishment this amazing girl nodded.

'Yes, that was my idea. I thought of going down to the quayside, and when I saw a ship that was going to Italy, I'd slip on board it when no one was looking. It would only take a few days, and I wouldn't eat anything, so it wouldn't be doing any harm, would it?'

The boy didn't answer, but stood staring down at his shoes for some minutes. Then he looked up at her with a pair of very direct grey eyes. Usually there was a hint of laughter in them, but at the moment they were quite serious.

'You know I don't think the stowaway idea is a very good one,' he pronounced.

'Oh!' – Rosanna was taken aback, and a little disappointed. She had thought it such a very good idea herself. But this boy, older than she was by at least two years, looked as if he knew what he was talking about, and she would have liked his approval. 'Why not?'

'Simple reason – ships to Italy don't sail from here,' said Iain Thompson. 'They sail from London Dock, or Southampton. In any case,' he added, seeing the dismay in her eyes, 'I don't think stowing away is a very good idea either. Stowaways have a pretty thin time, and they're usually discovered and brought back in deepest ignominy. Why don't you write to your friends in – wherever it is in Italy you live – and ask their advice. And, by the way, what exactly *did* happen this morning, if you don't think me awfully curious?'

Rosanna told him about the Mary Martin School, the ballet in which she was dancing the chief rôle, about the important persons who were going to be at the Evening of Ballet at Hordon Castle, her hopes (and Mary's too) of becoming a professional dancer.

'And now my chance is gone for ever!' she said sombrely. 'I know quite well that my aunt will never let me go to London for an audition to Sadler's Wells, so it's the end of my dancing career.'

'Oh, don't be so despondent,' said the boy. 'Another chance will come – they do if you keep hoping and working for it.'

Rosanna shook her head.

'No, I don't think another one ever will,' she said with a sigh.

'You've got the blues, that's what it is,' said Iain, 'sitting

137

here all by yourself. Tell you what, you beetle off down to the quayside and inspect the ships. If you find one going to Italy, you have my permission to stow away on board.' (He knew quite well that she would find no such ship, but she would be running her troubles out of her system.) 'But if you *don't* find one, you must promise to come back here, and I'll do my best to advise you.' His grey eyes filled with laughter. 'My advice is costly, I may tell you – a pound a word! All free to you, madame!' He made her a mock bow.

Rosanna had to smile, though it was a watery effort. Then her face fell.

'Oh, but my aunt wouldn't let you advise me. I mean she wouldn't let me even speak to you,' she said.

'Oh, dear! You *are* a defeatist!' laughed the boy. 'Why ask her? Come with me for a moment.' He took her by the arm and marched her through the house, out of the front door, and over the grass to the dividing hedge. 'Behold yon ancient bird's nest – well, if you care to leave a note addressed to me in there, I'll collect it and leave an answer for you – words of wisdom from a prophet!'

'All right,' agreed Rosanna. 'I promise.' After all, she thought, if there *wasn't* a ship she couldn't go, and that was that. But she intended to make sure of it, all the same.

Iain Thompson watched her walk away down the road.

'Graceful kid!' he thought once again. 'You'd know she was a dancer. Wonder what will happen to her? I'd like to have helped the kid. I'd have gone with her to look for her ship if I hadn't promised old Mackintosh to practise at the nets.' He pulled the branches of the hedge carefully over the old nest so that it couldn't be seen. Then he locked the door of Hayfield Lodge, replaced the key under the scraper, and returned to his own garden. As he picked up his cricket bag, he wondered when he would see Rosanna again.

As a matter of fact it was a very long time – five years exactly, and it was at Covent Garden, when she was dancing the Waltz from *Les Sylphides* (her first big rôle) at a matinée performance. He had just graduated from Oxford, and was having a few days' 'fling' in London before settling down to a job. As he watched the luminous figure on the stage, his thoughts went back to the moment when he had last seen Rosanna Corelli, a sad-eyed child, dressed in a washed-out cotton frock of an indefinite colour and no particular shape.

As for Rosanna, when she got to the end of the road, she turned and looked back. Iain was still there, standing by the hedge, and she waved to him. This, though of course she did not know it, was her last glimpse of Hayfield Lodge.

Chapter 13

His Majesty to the Rescue

Timothy Roebottom walked away from the yards whistling softly under his breath, and heaving a sigh of relief mentally. Royalty was always a bit of a strain, but it had gone off very well, all things considered. The Princess Tatiana had looked as lovely as any fairy-tale princess, and had captured the hearts of the Tynesiders with the warmth of her smile, and the gracious wave of her tiny white-gloved hand. Nevertheless Timothy was glad to hand them over to Dr Lishman, his boss, for a cup of tea. One was always a bit anxious at these sort of things (specially where foreign royalty was concerned), although of course there were masses of police everywhere, and quite a few detectives, not to mention the exiled king's private bodyguard – a dour fellow of the name of Hans Grootmann.

As for the young king himself, he seemed a nice enough chap, thought Timothy. He felt a sudden surge of pity for him. He had no job, no future, not even a country. He had been trained for kingship, and kingship alone. Now he had been flung high and dry by the wave of rebellion that had overwhelmed his country and swept away his throne, and there he would stay – like a bit of flotsam washed up by the tide – unless another wave came and swept him off again. Not very likely, thought Timothy as he strode along the quayside.

Oh, well, he'd be able to get off home now it was all over. His mother, he knew, would be bursting with curiosity to hear all about it. Funny how women seem to think foreign royalty romantic! Besides, he was going to a show tonight at Hordon Castle, away up north. It was a ballet show, and some of his very special friends would be dancing in it – a girl called Ella Rosetti, for one. She was world-famous now, of course, but he lost no chance of seeing her dance, even if he daren't think about her overmuch.

His thoughts were rudely interrupted by a crowd of people who came surging out of a narrow side street, nearly knocking Timothy over. Behind them came a long black car, and behind that another crowd of people.

'Oh, Lord!' said Timothy aloud. '*Them* again! Now what in the name of goodness are they doing down here?' Though he did not know it, the Princess Tatiana had suddenly expressed a desire to see an eighteenth-century house on the quayside, from the window of which a famous Northumbrian lady, Bessie Surtees, is said to have eloped with her lover, and the car was now on its way there. In fact, just as Timothy drew level, the car stopped in front of the house in question, and the royal visitors got out. The crowd surged forward, determined to get a closer look, and Timothy found himself squeezed against the wall. At the same moment he heard a muffled cry, and someone, or something, bumped violently against his ribs.

'Oh, I'm so s-sorry!' gasped a voice. 'They pushed me . . .'

Timothy looked down and saw, pressed close to him by the seething crowd, a little girl (about eleven years old he thought her) with large, dark, frightened eyes. Something about her struck a chord in his memory, and stabbed at his heart. She was like another little girl whom he had come across in a church in a pit village years and years before, and had befriended. She had the same scared, miserable look about her. Perhaps she was disappointed at not being able to see over the heads of the crowd – kids were funny that way. Always liked to see what was going on! He stooped, and swung her on to the windowsill of the warehouse behind them.

'There! Now you'll be able to see the fun,' he said.

'Oh, thank you,' said Rosanna. It was nice of him to help her, though she hadn't the least idea what she was supposed to look at. She had been making her way down to the quayside, and had suddenly found herself surrounded by this crowd of excited people. They seemed to be looking at a young man and a girl, who in their turn were looking at a house. They had their backs towards her at first, and then suddenly the young man turned round to climb back into the car, and Rosanna saw his face. She gave a gasp, and nearly fell off the windowsill in her astonishment.

'Leo!' she cried, almost unable to believe her eyes. 'Why, it's Leo! And Hans, too!'

The young man heard her voice, resonant as all Italian voices, and looked up.

'Why, it is my little friend, Rosanna Corelli!' he exclaimed in his turn. He was genuinely glad to see her. Inspecting shipyards, when you know less than nothing about them, is a dull business. He had had more than enough of it. He leant down towards Hans, his bodyguard, and at once that mysterious, silent figure cleared a way through the crowd.

141

Timothy told his mother all about it when he got home.

'It beat everything!' he said. 'The girl' – he had revised his opinion as to her age, and now thought her about twelve – 'jumped down from the windowsill where I'd parked her, and ran towards His Satanic Majesty – yes, that's the nickname they gave him at the works, and I must say it's rather apt – and then – I know you won't believe me, but it's gospel – he beckoned her into the royal car, handed his sister in, got in himself, and they drove away. Just like that! Now who on earth was the kid? You read stories about foreign titles washing up in hotels, or smuggling the crown jewels across the frontier out of the kingdom, so maybe this child was a member of the royal family of Slavonia (the Gionettis) who had escaped from the revolution. Mighty strange, though!'

Of course the evening papers were full of it. Each edition enlarged upon the one before, until they had built up a fantastic story. None of them, of course, hit upon the truth – it was much too simple!

Meanwhile the royal car was purring up the steep streets away from the quayside, and Rosanna was telling her new-found friend all about her life at Hayfield Lodge, her training with Mary Martin, and the ballet this evening in which she ought to have been dancing the principal rôle.

'And Veronica Weston, the world-famous *ballerina*, will be there,' she added, her eyes filling with tears at the thought of it, 'and Miss Rosetti too—'

'Miss Rosetti, did you say?' interrupted Leo, sitting up suddenly. 'You mean Miss *Ella* Rosetti?'

'Yes, and lots of other people as well. Jane Charlton – she used to be Jane Foster before her marriage – is going to dance—'

'Never mind about her,' ordered the young man imperiously. 'It is enough for me that Miss Rosetti is dancing. Come, we will go straight to this place which you call

Hordon, and you shall dance in your ballet.' He gave the order forthwith into a speaking-tube to the chauffeur.

'Oh, but my aunt—' faltered Rosanna. 'She will be furious.'

Leo looked up with such a scowl upon his handsome face that she stopped in dismay.

'If you aunt has done the things which you say she has done, then she is a veritable monster!' the young man declared. 'If this had been my country, I should have known just how to deal with that one. Here in England, however, justice is not meted out to such people as your aunt. All the same, we shall see that she does not "get away with it", as you say. I am learning the English language very fast, am I not? – nearly as fast as you, Rosanna!'

And then suddenly Rosanna knew who her friend was.

'Oh,' she said, 'I know now! You are this king of Slavonia that my uncle talked about – the royal person who was to inspect the shipyard. I suppose I ought to be calling you "Your Majesty"?'

'I am always just "Leo" to you,' said the young man, bowing as well as he could in the long, low car. 'This uncle you speak of – is he as diabolic as the outrageous aunt?'

'Oh, no,' said Rosanna. 'Uncle Tom was very kind to me – as kind as he dared, I'm sure. If it hadn't been for Uncle I should never have had any dancing lessons at all.'

'He shall be rewarded!' exclaimed Leo. 'I shall "put in a good word" for him. That expression is correct, is it not, Hans?'

'Quite correct, sir,' said Hans through the crack in the glass partition that divided the car into two parts.

All this time King Leopold's companion, the Princess Tatiana, had said not a word, but had sat staring at Rosanna. What on earth had her brother been up to now? She was too used to him, however, to ask questions, although she was dying to do so.

143

'Do you want me to come with you to Hordon?' she asked.

'Certainly,' said her despotic brother. 'You will be of the greatest use as a chaperone to my friend, Signorina Corelli here.' He bowed again to the little girl sitting opposite him in her faded cotton frock, with bare knees showing beneath her short skirt.

Chapter 14

The Evening of Ballet

To say that the company gathered together for the evening ballet performance was surprised when the black car with its coat of arms on the door panels, and the royal standard of Slavonia fluttering from its bonnet, drove up to the great iron-studded front door of Hordon Castle is putting it mildly. The news flew round like lightning that the exiled King of Slavonia and his sister, the Princess Tatiana (who was also the Duchess of Darlington) had come to watch the ballet. There was a little girl with them too, a very ordinary little girl—

'Why, it's Rosanna!' cried someone. 'Miss Martin! Miss Martin! Rosanna Corelli's here!'

Mrs Waybridge, who was arranging Monica's green *tutu*, looked up, unable to believe her ears. It couldn't be true – it just couldn't! How could Rosanna, whom she had left locked in Hayfield Lodge, possibly have got here? In any case, what on earth had Rosanna got to do with royalty? It must be a mistake. As for Mary Martin, she couldn't believe her ears either. It was quite too good to be true. She rushed out of the bedroom, which had been turned into a dressing-room for the dancers, and went swiftly downstairs to investigate. She found that it was indeed true. Rosanna was standing in the middle of the square-flagged hall, and with her were the royal visitors. Mary swept a low curtsy, graceful as only a ballet mistress can achieve. The young king held out his hand graciously for her to kiss. His sister bowed and smiled.

'I have heard all about you and your excellent school from my young friend here,' said Leopold, putting an arm affectionately round Rosanna's shoulders, to the delight of several ballet students who were peeping through the half-open door. 'I am very much looking forward to watching your performance this evening.' He looked down at Rosanna. 'You had better run away, had you not, my dear, and change into the beautiful costume you told me about. And now,' he added, turning back to Mary, 'if there is a room where my sister and I can sit down and rest until it is time for the ballet to begin, I should be grateful indeed – I so much detest crowds staring at me.'

Jane Charlton had appeared by this time and was in command of the situation.

'Certainly sir – madam,' she said. 'If you will be so good as to come this way. The library is quite empty, and I shall have coffee sent up to you immediately.'

The two royal personages (and, of course, the silent Hans) followed her up the shallow oak staircase, and into a beautiful sombre room with long mullioned windows. One of them was open, and through it you could see the delicate lace of a waterfall across the wooded dene on the edge of which the ancient castle stood, and hear the soft rustle and hiss of the water, as the breeze carried the sound.

'This will do splendidly,' said Leopold, sinking into a deep leather armchair. 'It is quite a beautiful room, is it not, Tatiana?'

'Indeed a lovely room,' echoed his sister.

'I shall leave you, then, for the moment,' said Jane. 'Is there anything else you would like?'

'Just one small thing,' answered Leopold. 'I wish you to send me the aunt of my little friend Rosanna. There are things which I have to say to this woman.'

As Jane said afterwards to Mary Martin, his voice when he made this request sent shivers running up and down her spine. It was like a hungry leopard who sees his dinner approaching! As for Mary, she was secretly delighted. When Bessie Waybridge had arrived with Monica, minus Rosanna, and had told her the tale about Rosanna's disobedience and subsequent punishment, her blood had boiled – not only out of pity for the child, but also for herself. She had choreographed this ballet with Rosanna in mind; she had coached Rosanna and cherished her. In her opinion the child had only to be seen by Veronica Weston and she would be at the Wells tomorrow. And now here was this stupid woman, Bessie Waybridge, putting her large, heavy foot right in the middle of her delicate plan and ruining it. But something had happened to change things. Rosannna, it seemed, had (unknown to anybody) influential friends, and her aunt was to be (as Thomas would have said) 'put on the mat'!

'Go along, Mrs Waybridge,' said Mary, trying to keep the note of glee out of her voice. 'His Majesty wishes to speak to you. It is about Rosanna, I gather. She seems to be a very special friend of his. Imagine her not telling us about him! . . . Now do hurry, Mrs Waybridge. I am sure there is not the least need for you to powder your face. His Majesty will never notice. Oh, and don't forget to curtsy.'

'Curtsy?' echoed Bessie.

'Yes, one must always curtsy to royalty,' Mary told her, not explaining to poor Bessie that a 'bob' would do. She had visions of stout Bessie Waybridge trying to achieve a full curtsy and the thought was nearly too much for her.

Bessie came out of the royal presence red up to the ears and weeping. It was obvious that His Majesty had let himself go. In fact, between ourselves, he hadn't enjoyed himself so much for a very long time!

'You were too bad, Leopold!' laughed Tatiana as the door closed behind Bessie. 'That poor stupid woman – you quite upset her.'

'I should hope I did,' answered Leopold, the scowl upon his face lifting a little. 'Imagine the agony she has caused that poor child, Rosanna – and she a friend of mine too. Nothing I could have said would have been too severe. I should have liked to cut off her head!'

Tatiana stared thoughtfully at her brother. Poor Leopold! He was so very intense. She herself was an English duchess, remember, besides being a princess of Slavonia. She had learned a little about the English and their sentimental ways during the years she had lived in her English castle. They just did not cut off people's heads any more. Moreover, she understood Leopold completely. He was not angry with Bessie Waybridge because she had behaved unkindly to a defenceless child, but because that child happened to be a friend of his. Hadn't he just said so?

The Princess Tatiana was right in her reasoning. As yet there was no spring of compassion in Leopold's heart, such as gushed out of Timothy Roebottom's when that young man saw anything young and defenceless, or old and feeble, being ill-treated. Timothy instantly went to the help of all defenceless things – whether a dirty crying child, a sad old horse struggling to pull a too-heavy load up a steep hill, a tortoise with a broken shell in a shop window (though he didn't particularly like tortoises), or indeed any suffering creature. When he saw a trembling old woman hesitating to cross the road, Timothy would straightaway offer her his strong young arm, however late he was, or where he was going. He wouldn't hurry her, either.

'Gently does it, granny!' he would say, as they reached

the far side. 'You O.K. now?' And off he would stride, his fair head six inches or so higher than everyone else's. A big, strong, gentle young man was Timothy Roebottom. A perfect knight Ella had called him, and it was true.

There was no doubt about it, thought Veronica Weston as she watched *The Emperor's Nightingale* – the little girl, Rosanna Corelli, was all that Mary Martin had said. But then her dear Mary was always right! That was why so many Wells dancers had received their first training from her. She had an unerring way of picking out potential *ballerinas*. Well, now she had done it again – this little girl must go to London at once. It appeared that she was older than she looked, so no time must be lost. The child's aunt would make no difficulties, Mary had just said. The young king of Slavonia had talked to her and she had agreed to everything. It only remained to find somewhere for her to stay, since there were no vacancies at the moment at White Lodge, the Sadler's Wells boarding school. Oh, well, something could be arranged, she was quite sure.

Veronica settled down to watch the ballet and was entranced. Mary was certainly a genius at choreography. Not for the first time she wished Mary could be persuaded to go to London, and become a choreographer there, but she knew it was useless. Mary felt she was doing more important work up here in the north of England, training all these girls, if not to be professional dancers, to be full of grace and health. And who knows – perhaps she was right. Next year, thought Veronica, her own little daughter Vicki should come to Mary for her very first ballet lessons. How strange to think of it! It seemed only yesterday that she herself had first seen the inside of Mary's studio. But this is life – things go round and round, people doing the same things in one generation after another. Her thoughts came back to the ballet. That child, Rosanna, how lovely she looked in the grey *tutu*, and how lyrical her dancing.

(As Monica had prophesied to her mother, Veronica saw no one else.) No wonder she defied death! No wonder the Emperor regained his health and happiness merely by listening to the beauty of her song! Here her thoughts were interrupted again by Mary, who came to warn her that after the next interval it was time for her to dance, and that she had better go and dress.

His Majesty of Slavonia was enchanted too. Although he had come primarily to see the beautiful Ella Rosetti, he nevertheless enjoyed watching his child-friend dance in her effective costume of the Real Nightingale. For one thing, she was very like Miss Rosetti in appearance, only of course many years younger . . . Ah, the ballet was ended. And now – he consulted his programme – Miss Veronica Weston would dance. She was giving them the *pas de deux* from *Swan Lake*, and a certain Toni Rossini was partnering her. A dark, dynamic young man (the world-famous Sebastian Scott, conductor-pianist, and Veronica Weston's husband) took his seat at the piano, and accompanied them faultlessly. Yes, he was certainly a magnificent pianist, thought the young man, who, like all Slavonians, was intensely musical. Moreover he was sympathetic, and obviously thinking about the dancers, as well as his own playing. Most unusual in anyone so famous!

The *pas de deux* had ended, and now came the moment the young man was waiting for – Miss Ella Rosetti would dance the famous waltz from the ballet *Les Sylphides*. Oh, how beautiful she was! His Majesty (though not many people would have agreed with him) thought her dancing surpassed even that of Miss Weston. Of course she was younger, and therefore more appealing, if less brilliant. As she danced, Leopold vowed afresh that he would speak to her this very night, that he would make her listen to him, and promise to be his bride. It must be so. He could not live without her.

★

Taking it all in all, it was indeed a memorable evening at Hordon Castle. His Majesty's chair had been placed so that he was screened from the common gaze, but at the end of the performance he had risen and bowed graciously to the audience, who incidentally were quite as interested in him as in the ballet!

We should like to be able to say that everyone was happy, but it wouldn't be true, because there was Bessie Way-bridge, whose Monica had been unnoticed by the high-ups, and whose frock (even her mother had to admit it) wasn't a patch on the beautiful creation worn by Rosanna. There was also Timothy Roebottom, whose thoughts were mixed. As he watched Ella dancing he was filled with joy and pride to think that this beautiful creature was the unhappy waif he and his mother had rescued from the dirt and squalor of Pit Street. And then he saw the young king of Slavonia talking to her after the performance, and his thoughts became sombre. They looked so suited to each other, the two of them. He supposed it was partly on account of their dark colouring. Anyhow, he felt that Ella had more in common with this handsome (if satanic) fairy-tale prince than she had with him – a poor engineer, living in an obscure, grey, north-country city. His income was six thousand pounds a year (compared to Leopold's sixty thousand, or was it six hundred thousand? It was all the same!) He hadn't even a home to offer her, and anyway one couldn't take a *ballerina* from Covent Garden stage and dump her down in a smoky industrial city for the rest of her days. It was like imprisoning a rare butterfly! No, for the present he must just forget about Ella as a girl, and merely enjoy her dancing as one of Sadler's Wells' greatest *ballerinas*. Later if ever he won a position enabling him to offer Ella the life she deserved, and if (as was extremely unlikely, thought Timothy) she was still free, he might dare to think about her again.

As for Ella herself, while she listened and talked politely

to His Majesty of Slavonia, she was thinking all the time about Timothy – dear Timothy, her hero, the curly-headed lad who had made her dream come true. Where had he gone? She had lost him amongst the crowd of people who surged round to congratulate her, and (it must be admitted) to get a close-up of His Satanic Majesty!

Chapter 15

A Proposal of Marriage

'And now, Ella,' said Leopold later in the evening, 'I have sent my sister home, and I am staying here at the Castle for the night' – he ignored Ella's horrified gasp – 'so that I may have a talk with you. Let us walk in the moonlight in these delightful gardens where we can be alone.' He had given strict orders that no one should be allowed to set foot in the gardens while he and Ella were there, though as a matter of fact no one would have dared to intrude. 'I want to know, Ella, why you have been avoiding me?'

Poor Ella was in a quandary here. One couldn't very well tell a young man (let alone a royal young man) that she was afraid of his proposing marriage to her, which was the plain truth, so she murmured something about being so very busy—

'Now you know, Ella, what you say is not the truth,' said Leopold, interrupting her. 'You run away from me because you are well aware that I wish to persuade you to become affianced to me – that I wish to make you my wife.'

'Oh, now you've said it!' exclaimed Ella. 'I do so wish

you hadn't, for you see, dear Leopold, although I like you tremendously,' (she almost added 'and am so very sorry for you', but stopped herself in time; that would have been a dreadful *faux pas*) 'I cannot possibly ever marry you.'

'There is someone else?' said Leo, drawing down his brows in a fine scowl.

A fleeting thought of Timothy came into Ella's mind, then she banished it. Timothy hadn't even come to congratulate her. He had gone home. It was obvious he didn't even remember her, let alone care for her – in that way.

'No,' she said, 'there is no one else, no one at all. But you see, Leopold, I am a dancer, and a dancer's life is dedicated to her art. She must not think of marriage—'

'Ah, but in my case it is different,' interrupted the young man quickly. 'You must know (indeed you do know) that in Slavonia there is an opera house – small, it is true, but grand. I am aware that, just now, I have no kingdom to offer you, and therefore no opera house—'

'Oh, stop! Stop!' cried Ella, full of pity. 'As if I care about that! Why, if you had nothing, and were the most ordinary person in the world and not a king at all, I shouldn't mind, but you see, dear Leopold, I don't love you.'

'That will come,' said His Majesty. 'Do not think that I shall let you go. I have a large fortune, and when you are on tour at the other side of the world, I shall follow you in my private plane. When you go to Europe, I shall go too. Every night that you dance at Covent Garden I shall watch you from my box, and wait for you in my car at the stage-door. I shall spend my life and my fortune watching you and waiting for you, Ella.'

'I can't stop you doing these things, of course,' said Ella, 'but it will be no use, no use at all. I'm a dancer, and nothing can alter that.'

'If you married me,' said Leo, making a last desperate

bid, 'you could have your own company. I would build for you a new opera house, grander than the one in Slavonia, on the shores of the Mediterranean. It would be in the grounds of our own estate, and we would ask all the most famous dancers in the world to dance in it. We would live in a pink-and-white château, and our garden would be fragrant with stephanotis and orange blossom, and outside our windows there would be an avenue of magnolia trees in which the nightingales would sing. There would be blue sky, and blue sea—'

'Oh, don't, please!' said Ella. 'You are making it so very difficult, offering me all this. You see, it can never, never be.'

'I shall wait for you,' declared Leopold. 'All my life I shall wait for you, my darling, and one day you will change your mind.'

'No, I never shall,' said Ella unhappily. He was really a dear boy, and she hated hurting him.

So here was a strange situation – two young men determined (for very different reasons) to wait for years and years – perhaps for ever – for this girl who was not even pretty, but who had captured their hearts with her gentle charm and the beauty of her dancing. The full moon shining serenely down on the towers and battlements of Hordon Castle smiled knowingly. It wasn't the first time! This same bright moon had seen strange things happen in the past within the walls of this hoary old border fortress. It had seen maidens carried off by Scottish maurauders, and maidens rescued. It had seen two maids in love with the same knight, and now here were two young men both wanting to marry the same girl. What a game, thought the moon! Which one would win? Perhaps it would be neither. Who knew?

Chapter 16

Rosanna Writes a Letter

We are nearing the end of our story. It only remains to let you look over Rosanna's shoulder and read a letter written a few days later to her friend, Anya Boccaccio, in Amalfi. It was headed:

> Carsbroke Place.
> London. W.1.

Dear Madame Boccaccio,

As you will see I am now in London. Oh, you don't know how lucky I've been! Of course it was Miss Martin's plan that began it all. She let me dance at her Evening of Ballet at Hordon Castle, and that was where Miss Weston saw me, and Miss Rosetti too. Well, they'd found out (I think Miss Martin told them, as a matter of fact) that I wasn't very happy at Hayfield Lodge, so there wasn't much point in my going back to it when I was joining the Wells immediately. There were my clothes, of course, but Miss Rosetti said that if they were all like the dress I was wearing, Aunt Bessie could send them to the parish jumble sale. She said she remembered what *she* felt like when she went to London in awful old clothes, and she wasn't having any other child feeling like that. So Mrs Charlton (who is a great friend of both Miss Weston and Miss Rosetti) let me stay at Hordon Castle, which is where she lives, and the day after the Evening of Ballet Miss Rosetti took me into Newcastle and bought me some new clothes. Oh, madame, she even bought me a hat – the first I've ever had!

You remember I told you about my lovely lace dress – the one Leo gave me – well, when Miss Rosetti heard about it, she insisted upon calling at 'Uncle's' (that's what the English call a pawnbroker), and do you know, he hadn't sold it yet, so Miss Rosetti bought it back. Wasn't it sweet of her? Oh, and when we were at 'Uncle's' we heard that poor Mrs Montessori had got over her operation, and would be home again before very long. We went to see her, and she was so pleased. She had been frightfully ill, and it had been 'touch and go', as they say here. I'm afraid I cried with happiness, and Miss Rosetti did too – out of sympathy she said. In some ways Miss Rosetti and I are very alike.

It seems odd to think that I probably shan't see Aunt Bessie ever again. I don't think I shall mind much and I'm quite sure *she* won't! I'm sorry, though, not to be able to say goodbye to Uncle Tom . . . he was kind to me sometimes, and it was through him that I went to Mary Martin's. Oh, and there was a boy who lived in the house next door (not the house joined on, but the one at the other side, if you see what I mean) who was very kind to me, and most sympathetic when I was trying to run away. He helped me to get back through the scullery window when I was hopelessly stuck. I should have liked to say goodbye to *him*.

Well, here I am in London! Miss Rosetti and I flew here on Monday, and it was my very first trip in an aeroplane. I am living at Lady Bailey's house – she is a rich old lady who loves the ballet so much, she does all she can to help dancers and make them happy by letting them live in her beautiful home. Next term I'm to have the Scott-Weston scholarship, but just now I'm Lady Bailey's guest, so she says. You don't know how kind everyone has been to me. And to think I nearly ran away (or rather *stowed* away on a ship) back to Italy, and now I wouldn't leave London for a *million* lire.

Tomorrow I join the Wells School. Think of it, Madame. What a romantic name, isn't it – the Wells! I don't think there is much more to say except goodnight, dearest Madame, and if you see Giorgio will you say I wish to be remembered to him. Above the noise of the London traffic, which is only a very faint roar from this house, I can hear Big Ben, and he has just chimed ten o'clock, so *buona notte*, and thank you for everything.

Your grateful pupil,

Rosanna Corelli.

Lorna Hill
A Dream of Sadler's Wells £2.50

This is the first of the Wells series in which we meet Veronica, who is determined to become a dancer. She is torn away from London and her ballet classes and sent to live with unsympathetic relations in Northumberland, but she manages to overcome all sorts of setbacks and finally reaches her audition for the Royal Ballet School at Sadler's Wells.

Veronica at the Wells £2.50

Veronica is now at the Sadler's Wells ballet school and her first days are exciting, even a little frightening for not everyone welcomes the talented newcomer. When she is fifteen, Veronica has the most wonderful Christmas present – her first part at Covent Garden.

Lorna Hill
No Castanets at the Wells £2.25

After meeting the exciting young Spanish dancer Angelo Ibanez, Caroline Scott is even more determined than ever to take her dancing seriously. Eventually she follows her talented cousin, Veronica Weston, to the Sadler's Wells Ballet School. Once there, however, she becomes the despair of her teachers – all except the fierce and fiery Serge Lopokoff, for it is only in his Character classes that Caroline really comes alive. Fortunately, Angelo has never forgotten the promise he made that Christmas in Northumberland . . .

Masquerade at the Wells £2.25

Jane and Mariella Foster were cousins, with everything and nothing in common – Mariella, daughter of a prima-ballerina, loved horses and dogs and the outdoor life that Jane was forced to lead. Jane was prepared to do anything for the ballet lessons which her cousin hated. A daring deception is born when Jane takes Mariella's place at an audition for Sadler's Wells Ballet School. She passes and begins a new life – as Mariella Foster! Jane loves the Wells, but fears that one day – someone will discover her secret . . .

Jane Leaves The Wells £2.50

When Veronica Weston marries Jane Foster steps into several of her roles – gaining instant success and admiration. Her future as a ballerina seems assured, but Jane distrusts her own good fortune, knowing that, unlike Veronica, she is not one of the 'great ones'. During an eventful midwinter visit to Scotland Jane is faced with an almost impossible choice – her dancing or her love for a rugged Northumbrian, Guy Charlton.

Ella at the Wells £2.50

When Ella Sordy – foundling from the back streets of a northern mining village – stepped out on the stage for the very first time, she had nothing in common with the *prima ballerina* of the Sadler's Wells except her childhood dreams of becoming a dancer. But Veronica Weston herself is in the audience and decides, there and then, to become 'fairy godmother' to the naturally gifted girl . . .